Arbor Day Can Be Deadly

A Bucket List Mystery Novella

Ryan Rivers

Published by Partners in Crime Press LLC
320 Gold Ave SW Ste 620 PMD 2041
Albuquerque, NM 87102

Visit www.ryanriversbooks.com

*For my son
with love (always!)*

Chapter 1

MY RIGHT EYE TWITCHED, yet I couldn't look away from the flickering lights of the Wild West Airlines sign.

"Doesn't it make you want to scream?" I asked.

"Mr. Tanaka?"

I stretched my neck past the customer service rep, searching for a loose plug. Perhaps she'd let me climb over the counter and fix it myself. "I bet bugs get back there too, don't they? And die."

"Mr. Tanaka?"

I tried looking at her, but the light flutters kept pulling my focus. My eyes landed on her name tag: Chanterelle.

Chanterelle? Was that a name? I was pretty sure it was a

mushroom. I'd ask my sister Jenny; she was the chef in the family. Did Chanterelle's parents have backup names? Did someone lose a bet?

"Mr. Tanaka!?"

The squeak of wet shoes scraping against tile interrupted my contemplation. Chanterelle wore a bright orange dress with big white buttons and an even bigger cowgirl hat. Her skin also glowed orange, an unfortunate result of the overhead lighting mixed with the glare from her computer screen.

I counted, 1-2-3, and forced a smile. "Apologies. What was the question?"

She lit up like a jack-o'-lantern when she read off the screen. "You arrived here from . . . Seattle?"

I knew that. I was there. Was that a trick question? I nodded anyway.

"And Austin is your final destination?"

"Yes. No. Well, sort of. My sister's picking me up here. It's a short drive to the town where she lives."

"You checked your bag in Seattle?"

I pinched out a smile that felt more serial killer than patient customer. "Yes . . . that's where I live. My bag and I left together."

Chanterelle missed my facial contortions as she tapped on her keyboard. "Based on the tracking information, your bag might be in Los Angeles?"

"Might be?"

"It probably didn't make the connecting flight?"

Was this a guessing game? "Probably?"

A crash reverberated through the terminal, causing me to jump. The man behind me waved an apology and picked up his overturned bag. I'd already pegged him as the squeaky shoe offender, so I responded with another pinched smile.

I turned back to the airline rep, my fingers digging into the counter. And counted. 1-2-3. 1-2-3.

"Look, uh, Chanterelle . . .?"

Her face brightened with recognition.

"My bag is lost, and for reasons I think are obvious, I want it. I can't allot any more time for 'Airport Miscellaneous.'"

She stopped typing. "Airport what?"

I spun around my homemade travel itinerary. "'Airport Miscellaneous.' It's one of my travel categories. See? Five minutes for unnecessary, but socially polite chitchat with the baggage handler. Another forty-five minutes for security. I gave myself a ten-minute buffer there, but I wore slip-on shoes and no belt, so it only took me thirty minutes. I allotted ten minutes for a green tea to decompress from the unnecessary, but socially polite chitchat. Anyway, you clearly see I literally have no time for more time." I pointed for emphasis. "It's not on the schedule."

"But you saved fifteen minutes with security!"

I sighed, diverting my gaze to the unimpressive-looking terminal. I thought everything was supposed to be bigger in Texas. Concrete columns, the girth and texture of tumors, propped up this prison. A handful of passengers circled the baggage carousels, their shoes squeaking as they squabbled over whose nondescript black roller bag was whose. If this place represented where my sister had moved, it would be a quick visit.

"Mr. Tanaka, our travel app will alert you when your bag arrives. Hopefully, it'll be on the next plane."

I propped my elbows on the counter so I could tug a healthy clump of hair. "Hopefully? Isn't this your airline's guarantee?" I read the Wild West Air slogan from my boarding pass. "'We'll Git You There. Darn Tootin.'"

"And you're here!" When Chanterelle held out her arms, I got a whiff of her perfume de burnt coffee.

"But my bag's not. And the peanut promised."

"The peanut?"

My fingers flicked the cardboard cartoon cutout facing me.

"Your spokespeanut . . . person. This thing wearing spurs and lassoing an airplane."

"That's a goat, sir."

I squinted at the cutout. "Are you sure?"

"A baby goat. Billy the Kid."

I blew air from my nose. "Perhaps Billy ate my bag?"

"He's not a real goat." Chanterelle giggled.

"He's not? But he sang and danced his way through my inflight entertainment?"

"That's Levi Blue."

"Levi who?"

"Levi Blue. He voices Billy the Kid."

I blinked.

Chanterelle gasped and raised her hands to her mouth. "You don't know Levi Blue? The actor? The star of *Tween of the Crime*?"

"Tween of the what? Are you just saying random words?" I caught my reflection in the metal counter that I gripped. I was used to seeing myself in unflattering light. The overhead lights in my Seattle ICU augmented the pink undertones in my bone-colored skin, but at least I appeared cheerier to patients. Now, in this dinky little airport, my skin looked sallow, my veins almost green. I was bloated, too, no doubt the result of my recent late-night snacking. Since my leave from the hospital, I'd consumed more than the occasional glass of red wine. Tufts of coarse black hair spiked in various directions along my scalp. It had a messy appearance some guys would spend an hour to achieve. Altogether, I resembled one of those beady-eyed ghosts that crawled out of wells in Japanese horror movies.

I gave Chanterelle a small smile. "I don't expect you to understand, but I've had a miserable few months. Job, personal life, all of it, all miserable. And now I've lost my things. I have no things, Chanterelle. I am thing-less. I'm also a tad anxious, as

I'm sure you can tell." An involuntary laugh escaped my mouth. "I haven't seen my sister in three years. Three!"

Chanterelle reached under the counter and pushed a tote bag toward me.

I exhaled. "What's this?"

"Toothbrush, toothpaste, razor, comb. Now you have things!"

I studied the clear plastic on the side of the tote. "Is this a Billy the Kid lapel pin?"

"And your official Wild West Air postcards. Send those to all your friends in Seattle. Show 'em what a good time you're having."

The image on the top postcard was a powdery white sand beach with palm trees swaying lazily. I doubted this scene would greet me when I left the terminal. "Is this where all your lost baggage vacations?" I laughed at my joke.

It was Chanterelle's turn to blink. "Maybe grab a granola bar before you leave, or a banana? Might help your blood sugar."

Darn Tootin.

Chapter 2

A WHOOSH OF HUMIDITY BLASTED ME when the automatic doors opened. My first Texas facial. Jenny was already waiting, leaning against a car. My stomach dropped, and the simultaneous urge to run and hide planted me where I stood. A few passengers stepped around me, eliciting an amused grin from my sister.

I finally moved, my face yanked into a tight smile, my hand clutching the tote. She wore a white, off-the-shoulder top with lace on the sleeves, teal pants because Jenny needed her color pop, and cream and white two-tone heels.

"Sho-chan." Her nickname for me. She wrapped her arms

around me and drew me into a hug. I stood rigid, but then rested my chin on the top of her head. Jenny had swept her hair back and fastened it with an antique barrette from our *Obachan*, or grandmother. It was crafted from vintage kimono silk, and the pattern included green, orange, and cream hexagons. Jenny eventually let go of me, adjusted my black blazer, and knitted her brows. "What's wrong with your face?"

"I'm smiling," I said through my teeth.

She smoothed her fingers over my cheeks to relax the muscles. "There. I thought you got some shoddy Botox. I didn't want to lie about how 'fresh' and 'lifelike' you looked." From a key fob, Jenny unlocked her car, a blinding green two-door hatchback.

"Yikes. It's a key lime on wheels," I said.

"Excuse me? It's adorable, and you know it. It's called Grassy Meadow, but I like key lime. What do you think?"

"Zesty."

She eyed the tote. "No luck with your luggage, huh? You didn't lecture anyone, did you?"

"I offered constructive criticism for improved efficiency."

Jenny wagged her finger and deepened her voice. "This was not a scheduled part of Airport Miscellaneous."

"That's a terrible impression of Ma," I deadpanned.

She stuck her tongue out at me before sliding into the car.

I cracked some tension from my neck, shrugged off my blazer, and folded it over my forearm. I sucked in one big breath before tugging on the door handle. When I sat down, my knees pushed against the dash. I pinched a muscle straining for the seat belt and then smoothed the blazer across my lap when I was settled.

"You can just throw that in back," Jenny said.

I pulled the blazer closer and massaged its pocket. I'd began the day with four antidepressants, but popped one on the way to the airport, and the second when the plane hit turbulence. The unscheduled bag episode drove me to take the third. With the status of my bag TBD, I only had one pill in case of an emergency.

Jenny adjusted her cat-eye sunglasses and shifted into drive, neglecting to look for cars until she pulled out in front of one. An oncoming driver alerted her with a tap of his horn, which Jenny interpreted as a greeting. She tooted in reply as we zipped out of the terminal. We made a few quick turns before merging onto an interstate.

"Only a forty-five-minute drive, give or take," she said.

I fiddled with the metal buttons of my blazer, studying the concrete sound walls that surrounded us. "That's faster than I thought."

"Smack between Austin and San Antonio, a straight shot down I-35."

"I see it's been raining a lot here." I'd prepared a list of neutral topics for the car ride: weather, food and drink, and travel. I didn't need a sisterly grilling while locked in a moving vehicle. I also wanted to avoid any volatile conversations with Jenny. For example, why did you quit school for the second time, or were you possessed when you bought a café in Armpit, Texas?

"There's still some flash flooding in the area, but it's drying up," Jenny said, following my plan. "Should be clear for the festival tomorrow."

"Oh, there's a festival? That's nice."

I heard a dramatic sigh from the driver's side. "I told you all this when you invited yourself here," she said. "We have the Arbor Day Festival tomorrow. I'm making some small bites and mixing cocktails to promote the café. You even agreed to help."

"Of course, I remember now." Actually, I'd recalled little of the last two weeks. Things kind of went dark and numb when the hospital placed me on leave. The news blindsided me, and I didn't even remember the sequence of events that led me to call

Jenny for a visit. "Shall I bust out my bartending moves?" I asked, attempting to return to the approved list of small-talk topics.

Jenny snorted, and her infectious smile returned. "No, no, you shan't. You can carry supplies and mingle with the locals. You can be social for an hour. Right?"

"I won't hug people, but, for you, I'll hug trees."

"That's actually supposed to be good for you, hugging trees. Makes you happy, releases some chemical."

"Oxytocin. And that's a myth."

"Well, the festival is a big deal. It's held on the town square, and the poppies are in full bloom. It's all a nostalgic throwback to the show."

I watched the airport hotels whoosh by as we increased speed. "What show?"

"*Tween of the Crime*? Levi Blue?"

Those ridiculous names again. "Have you been hanging out with Chanterelle?"

"The mushroom?"

"Thank you!"

Jenny tugged at her ear. "Anyway, they filmed a two-part Arbor Day episode in Bluebonnet Hills. It's a classic. Let's see, there was the big tap dance number in the chicken processing plant, the cow tipping dream sequence, the psychedelic shootout at the Red Poppy Corral . . ."

"Was this show a comedy? Horror?"

"A bit of everything. I can't believe you've never seen it."

"I can't believe *you* have. We grew up in the same household."

"But I made friends. A skill you never mastered."

"It's on my bucket list."

"Well, I made friends who watched TV. Levi's character solved crimes and restored tween justice." She snuggled into her chair. "I guess it all sounds cooler when you're a giggly, awkward eleven-year-old."

"The place you moved to throws a party for a child actor?"

"We're celebrating the town, not the actor. The show was cancelled years ago. Levi's old now—like, your age."

"So, early thirties?"

"Exactly."

I tried to relax my mind and focus on the outside noise: the hum of the engine, the steady thump of tires on asphalt, the rattle of my window. Jenny zigzagged between lanes, maneuvering around eighteen-wheelers and eventually settling on the far-right lane. She set the cruise control, and I winced at the number of cars only several hundred feet in front of us.

"How's work?" she asked.

Not an approved topic. I knew these questions would come, but I hadn't prepared satisfactory answers. Lying wasn't an option, but neither was telling the truth. "Work is work," I said. There. Nailed it.

"And Vicky? How's she?"

I bit the inside of my cheek. "Fine. Busy." Victoria hated the shortened version of her name. Jenny knew that.

"You two set a date yet?"

"Still coordinating schedules." I pretended to be interested in the happenings outside my window. The industrial landscape of blah and meh transitioned into more green spaces that were dotted with colorful flowers. One flower, about a foot high and bursting with silky-haired leaflets of blues, purples, and white flecks, caught my attention. "What are the blue ones called?"

Jenny turned in my direction, the hatchback swerving with her. "Bluebonnets, the state flower."

I nodded, connecting the name of the flower with Jenny's new home in Bluebonnet Hills.

She continued. "People here are obsessed with them. For real, they'll literally stop in the middle of the road and throw their kids into a patch for a photo."

I smiled—a real one this time. "That sounds familiar. I guess bluebonnets are to Texas what cherry blossoms are to Japan." As children, our family visited Tokyo annually for *hanami*, or our cherry blossom viewing.

"Funny you make that connection." After a few minutes of silence, Jenny burst out laughing. "Remember the time Ma pushed us into the moat just to snap a photo?"

I chuckled, recalling the experience. Ma placed Jenny and me on a boat along the Chidorigafuchi path, right under some branches of cherry blossoms. The photo captured me laughing at Jenny's wailing.

That was a happy time, and it would be nice to see that photograph again.

The indigos and violets of the bluebonnets blurred as we whizzed past them. "That was our last family trip to Japan," I said.

"I can't believe I let Ma cut my bangs straight across like that." She lifted a hand from the steering wheel to make finger scissors. "Fifteen years goes by fast, eh?" She nodded to the glove compartment. "Open it up. Read above the fold."

I followed her instructions and pulled out a newspaper. The masthead announced itself as the *Bluebonnet Bee* and above the fold was a photo of Jenny and the headline, "Cherry Blossom Café Cooks Up Texas Favorites with Japanese Flair."

"*Sakura*." The Japanese word for cherry blossoms and Jenny's middle name. I touched the image of my grinning, waving sister in front of a building that looked as grimy as the newsprint it was printed on. "This is why you quit culinary school?"

The hatchback jerked. "And we were having such a tender family moment," Jenny said.

"Only asking a question."

"There's a sharp edge to your *question*." She took her hands off the steering wheel to make air quotes. The car drifted near the ditch.

I grabbed the handle above my door. "The decision seemed impulsive, that's all. You'd never even been to Texas."

"So what? I got a ridiculous deal on the café, and people love my food. I'm experimenting in ways I couldn't in culinary school."

"But why do that here?"

"I like it here, Sho. I like the people. And I'm in a perfect location for foodies. Lots of people drive through Bluebonnet Hills."

"Yes, on their way to somewhere else."

"That will change when the town revitalization is complete."

I laughed. "When will that be?"

"About the time you and Vicky perform the wedding march." Jenny shot me some side eye.

I adjusted my body away from her. "The family was a little surprised by your choices, that's all."

"Exactly. My choices. Coloring outside the lines has its advantages. You should try it sometime, Mr. Structure."

I folded my arms. "Noted."

"And Ma will get over it. She doesn't think you need a degree to cook, anyway. Meanwhile, I'll happily soak up her silent treatment."

"But all that attention redirects to me."

"The tiniest violin. The sad life of the favorite child. Is that why you're here? Did Ma send you?"

"Of course not." I spotted the sign that welcomed me to Bluebonnet Hills. I squinted to read the town motto: "Where Every Day is Arbor Day." I worked to decipher that code when my body flew forward. My knees gouged into the dash right before the seat belt yanked me back.

Jenny growled and bopped the steering wheel. I followed her line of sight to the stopped car. A motorist stood, phone in hand, attempting to bribe his golden retriever to sit in a patch of bluebonnets for a photo op.

Jenny leaned back in her seat. "Welcome to Texas."

Chapter 3

THE THIRD EMAIL from the human resources department at my Seattle hospital included the same gobbledygook as the first two.

I shifted in the swivel chair at the lunch counter of the Cherry Blossom Café. Jenny had delivered a dinner plate of beef omurice. Think Western omelet meets Japanese fried rice. But food could wait.

The email included all the standard hits: "failure to perform the required functions of your position . . .," "failure to complete duties outlined in your job description . . .," "failure to comply with your mandatory counseling . . ."

Failure, failure, failure. Blah, blah, blah.

My pointer finger hovered over the trash can icon, but I stopped to read the last paragraph, which threatened termination if I "failed" to seek counseling within thirty days. Huh. Well, that was new.

"You're not eating." Jenny hovered across the counter.

I almost dropped the phone onto my plate. "Sorry, got distracted." I took a moment to appreciate the omurice. Jenny had seasoned it with furikake, and breathing in the earthy mix of sesame and seaweed filled my body with nostalgia and tugged at my taste buds. The pillowy egg omelet, the size of the eight-inch skillet it was cooked in, draped over the mixture of jasmine rice, ground beef, carrots, and peas; drizzled with thick katsu sauce; and dotted with dark scallion greens. Topping any dish with greens elevated its curb appeal, a foodie tip I had learned from Jenny. You eat with your eyes, and green makes everything pop. The taste matched its look—rich beef, tender veggies, salty katsu, crunchy rice. I took a breath between forkfuls and said, "This is umami-licious."

Her shoulders relaxed. "Now do you understand why I came here? Bought this café?"

I pushed back against the vinyl swivel chair, wiping my mouth to hide my grimace. The café certainly had the beginnings of a distinct personality. The L-shaped lunch counter was a romantic throwback to gathering and community. I'd also noticed my sister's Tansu wood step chest in the corner. It was a piece of furniture she'd shipped around the country, no matter where she lived. She'd displayed a few trinkets on each of the five steps, a metal dish in the shape of Texas, a vase stuffed with wildflowers, her embroidered koi fish jewelry box. I thought fusing Japanese and Texas décor would make my eyes bug, but Jenny deserved some credit. The natural woods, accented by brassy hardware, added some warmth. Even the rustic Texas star complemented the adjacent watercolor triptych of a Japanese mountain landscape. My sister understood fusion, whether it was with her food or her design aesthetic.

I raised my fork for another bite. No, I still didn't understand. Perhaps the place would grow on me, but I didn't see that happening in the four days and three nights I had left in Bluebonnet Hills.

I was spared the awkward exchange thanks to a customer who stood beside me. She was one of three diners making up this evening's "dinner rush."

She spoke to Jenny in a voice that reminded me of stale cigarettes. "Cash is on the table. I subtracted the seven percent discount from my bill."

Seven percent discount? Did I hear that correctly? That was an extravagant policy for a high-risk business. I sliced some egg with the edge of my fork. Jenny never managed money well. I'd sit down tomorrow and review her business plan. If she had one.

"Thanks, Miss Odessa," Jenny said. "See you tomorrow afternoon at the festival."

I glanced up and noticed the woman glowering at me. She looked around sixty, but everything about her—mouth, cheeks, eyes—was pinched. Her dirty-dishwater brown hair was pulled into a tight bun, except for two white strands that framed her face, one on each side of her head.

"Oh, this is my big brother, Sho," Jenny said. "He's visiting from Seattle."

I bowed in her direction. "Howdy."

Her cornflower-blue eyes were striking, but the way she used them for surveillance made me squirm. I pulled my blazer closed, pushing against my bellyful of beef omurice. A few excruciating eye flicks later, the woman grunted and shuffled away.

Jenny leaned across the counter and got in my face. "Howdy?"

"What? It's a greeting."

"Snob."

"Seven percent discount?" I asked, moving right along.

The fluorescent lights above picked up the shadows under Jenny's eyes. "I have this buggy POS system. I give an itty-bitty discount to encourage customers to pay cash." She held two fingers slightly apart to illustrate how little ittybitty was. "It's been great for business."

I opened my mouth to respond, but she raised her hand.

"The whole business side of running a café is coming. Slowly. I might take a class or two in the fall." She glanced at me. "You know budgeting and math are not my strengths."

Oh, I knew. "Ma still wears black over that tragedy."

"So I didn't meet the family expectations and become an engineer or scientist." She held her hands up. "Sue me."

"Ma's always encouraged your interest in food."

Jenny released a pop of air. "Like forcing me to major in food science? Food. Science." She held out each hand as if revealing a magic trick. "I mean, can you imagine? Microbiology, chemistry, making protein bars from crickets?" Jenny gave a small smile, half amused, half defeated. "Only Ma could take the fun out of food. Of course, you, The Amazing Sho-chan, went into medicine and saved the family from scandal and ruin."

I pushed away my plate. "Nursing wasn't on the family's list of approved medical professions, I assure you. Especially for the eldest son."

My parents never openly disapproved of my career, but it took a lot of painful explanation to convince them that nursing wasn't only for failed medical students. There were also a few indirect and wildly amusing conversations about my sexuality. I was dating Victoria then, but I wondered if my parents thought nursing was a gateway to some bigger lifestyle change. In the end, I had their unwavering support and lots of cheering at my graduation. It occurred to me that my parents were perhaps harder on Jenny because my career choices caught them by surprise. We had a middle brother too, but, well, I doubted any pressure was applied there.

"Tell me how all this came about." I waved my fork in the air. "How did you end up owning a café in Texas?"

"It all started with the theme dinner at culinary school. You know, the ones we did with the hotel/restaurant management students?"

I vaguely remembered an invitation when Jenny was head chef. But a quick flight from Washington state to New Jersey wasn't workable. I kept my expression neutral as I sensed Jenny was baiting me.

"Sorry, course you don't know, you never came to a theme dinner."

Ding ding ding. If only I won medals for these Passive Aggressive Olympics.

"Well, Fredrich Ernst, the town mayor, ended up at my dinner, and that's when I learned about the café."

"How does the mayor of Bluebonnet Hills end up in Claremont, New Jersey?"

"He used to be a US congressman in the state, before he got elected mayor."

I raised an eyebrow. "What dirty scandal got him from DC to here? Naughty photos? Campaign finance fraud? Naughty photos of campaign finance fraud?"

"Bluebonnet Hills is his hometown. He actually wanted to give back to his community. Anyway, they loved my menu, they loved my take on Southern cuisine, and they were scouting fresh talent to help revitalize the town."

"They? The mayor and who else?"

"His wife, Aviva. Loved my short ribs. She's actually the mayor now."

"Hmm. Is job swapping a Texas tradition?"

She rolled her eyes. "It's all strange and sad, really. Fredrich disappeared four months ago, right after I arrived here. The town council appointed Aviva acting mayor until the next election."

I rubbed my hands together. "The plot thickens. And this place was also a café before you bought it?"

Jenny nodded. "The Greasy Spoon. Isn't that a horrible name? Anyway, the guy that owned it, Javi—he manages most of the commercial property in town—thought he could run a restaurant too."

"I assume he failed?"

"Spectacularly. Sold this place at a loss, said it was a win-win. I get the café on the cheap, he scores a tax break."

I ran a hand over my face. "Just so I understand. A small-town Texas mayor happened to be in New Jersey for your culinary school theme dinner and happened to be looking for a new chef with a twist on Southern cuisine? You secured this place well below market value because the previous owner wanted a write-off?" I sat back in my chair. "Did I get all that?"

"Just a series of happy coincidences." Jenny smirked.

I balled the paper napkin and set it on my plate. "Thank you for dinner, but I better get to bed." Jenny lived above the café.

She stared at the floor for a moment before making eye contact. "You'll help tomorrow? With the festival setup?"

I nodded as the café's line cook appeared behind the kitchen serving window.

"Jenny? The sink faucet is leaking again. Can you make a call?"

She checked her watch. "On it." She walked toward the saloon-style doors that separated the dining room from the kitchen. As she passed through, I heard a crack and then watched a door strip from its hinges. Jenny's head slumped. "One more thing for the repair list."

LISTENING TO THE BUZZING and whirring from the ceiling fan in my bedroom relaxed me. I tapped on the Billy the Kid icon for the Wild West Airlines app, searching for a luggage update. Levi Blue. I chuckled at Billy's toothy grin. I hoped that was a stage name.

No update on the bag. Groan. I grabbed the T-shirt and sweatpants that Jenny had found for me and set the phone on the bedside table. Jenny had somehow snagged our family's *kusuri tansu,* or medicine chest. The Hinoki wood chest stood about thirty-two inches high, with fifteen tiny square drawers stacked in rows of three, hand-carved with Japanese characters. The Tanaka siblings spent countless childhood hours hiding toys and candies in those drawers, each taking a turn, opening one at a time, hunting for the hidden treasure. I stuck a finger through one of the rounded handles and pulled, anticipating a surprise but getting a whiff of linseed instead. Jenny relished in her role as the family rebel, but she showed a deeper connection to our upbringing and culture than me or our brother.

I'd snapped the elastic of the sweatpants around my waist when my phone dinged, alerting me to a text message. I slipped under the quilt to read the message from Dr. Elena Gorga. Dr. Gorga was a colleague, who wanted to know how I was doing. I'd recently caught her in a distracted moment and finessed her into writing me a stronger Zoloft prescription. My psychologist had prescribed the lowest dosage of 25 milligrams when I clearly needed more. A few weeks prior, the unstable ex-husband of a patient had pulled a gun on me. At least, I thought it was a gun. The incident left me jittery, and my assigned psychologist diagnosed me with post-traumatic stress.

Prescription medication helped, and I understood dosing and monitoring side effects. Even if I took both prescriptions, I'd be under the recommended daily dosage. But I wasn't so lucky with my second request. Dr. Gorga reported me to my psychologist, who bored me with psychobabble, using words like "trigger" and "self-care" and "mindfulness." Before I knew it, the hospital administrator "invited" me to her office for a "critical conversation" about how the trauma was affecting my performance. It was all very HR, neatly packaged and tied with a big red bow.

Before I stepped into the hospital administrator's office, I'd noticed the security guard roaming the halls. His uniform strained against his midsection, and the enthusiasm for his job was so flaccid that he barely lifted his shoes to walk. The details seemed inconsequential until I noticed the administrator kept her office door open. Rather than lecture me from behind her desk, she moved to the chair next to mine. Classic HR maneuver: reduce the power dynamic to limit the likelihood that I'd go bananas and drop-kick a potted plant. As she spoke, I heard the shuffling of the guard's shoes every few minutes. Another HR maneuver: as a precaution, alert the authorities to a sensitive meeting where the outcome was unknown.

How had I gone from being a respected ICU nurse to an uncontrollable druggie prowling for his next fix? I wasn't an IV drug user, shooting up between shifts, or stealing patients' medication. Though the latter became more tempting than I had calculated.

The administrator spoke in soft, composed tones, aggravating the situation, because all I heard was the guard who refused to pick up his feet. I wondered how they would have coped with my long hours, the inconsistencies in shift schedules, or having a weapon waved in their face. That would give anyone PTSD. But before I could engage, the administrator had placed me on leave for an undetermined amount of time. The psychologist agreed to a higher dosage of meds to manage the titration process, in exchange for more therapy. The meeting's outcome left me numb, but no potted plants were harmed.

Thinking about that meeting still made my arms prick and my neck ache. Or perhaps those were the effects of the Zoloft withdrawal. I kicked off the quilt, which felt like a rough, restrictive blanket. Dr. Gorga seemed genuinely concerned. Still, my reply could wait until morning.

I activated my phone's "do not disturb" feature, clicked off the lamp, and stared at the ceiling. It was both easy and depressing to just up and leave my apartment for a trip to Texas. No sick days to request. No fiancée to tell. No pets to board. No plants to water. I put my mail on hold to feel less pathetic. I'd have a pile of junk mail to look forward to, waiting for me to throw away.

I fidgeted with my hands, feeling for the quilt again, uninterested in sleep. Sleep only brought nightmares and night sweats. But if this town's motto was accurate, and every day was Arbor Day, today was also tomorrow, making sleep nonessential. I watched the blades of the fan spin, chuckling at my joke. At least I could amuse myself.

Chapter 4

THE PREP FOR THE ARBOR DAY FESTIVAL involved me lugging five trays of small bites, four trays of white chocolate almond bark, three boxes of plastic utensils, two boxes of booze, and a partridge in a pear tree to the Bluebonnet Hills Square. Once we arrived, Jenny pointed and shouted orders as she scrawled a menu on the chalkboard she'd also made me carry.

After I'd unpacked the last box, I slipped on my blazer. I still wore my travel clothes, but I'd hung everything in the shower that morning for a DIY steam job. Jenny rewarded my work with a cocktail. I held up the red concoction for an inspection.

"It's called Very Cherry Smashed. I mixed tequila, cherries, orange liqueur . . . It's booze, not a lab sample. Drink up."

And I did. The sourness of the lime hit my tongue first, but it was cooled by the freshness of orange and then walloped with the tart cherry. Anything cherry reminded me of cough syrup, but the tequila mellowed the flavors. "This tastes pretty good."

"I might die from the faint praise."

I toasted her with my plastic cup. "You sure you don't need me to stay?"

"Nope. I got one of the high school guys to help serve. You go soak in some of this Texas culture." She pointed to the center of the square. "The mayor is hosting a program at the courthouse."

I sipped my drink for courage and wandered toward the gathering crowd. The courthouse stood in the center of the town square, surrounded by Victorian-era storefronts that resembled a Dickens-inspired Christmas village; multistory, colorfully painted brick buildings with canted bay windows and turrets. Besides Jenny's café, there was a winery, gift shop, florist, and lots of "For Lease" signs hanging in the lower-level windows. The center of the square was landscaped with clipped grass accented by wild native grasses that popped with color from the wildflowers and hugged by the gnarled branches of the live oaks that towered above.

Performing under one of those trees was a lanky yellow-haired man, about my age, wearing a black-and-white striped turtleneck and black beret. A gaggle of middle-aged women surrounded him, hooting and clapping.

He held out his hands, moving one at a time. I realized he was miming, trapped in an imaginary box. But without the white-face makeup, he resembled a cartoon cat burglar. Crazy Mime did a pratfall on the grass, much to the ladies' delight. He had a knack for physical comedy, an agility that reminded me of those 1960s sitcom actors who tripped over furniture during the opening credits. He should lose the beret, though. He popped up, flashed a lopsided grin, and soaked in the rapturous applause from his fans. Was that a catcall whistle?

The echoes from an amplified voice grabbed my attention, and I turned to the courthouse. Mime Time indulged my camp sensibilities, but I hoped the mayor had a more cultured program. The amplified voice grew louder and clearer as I moved toward the steps of the courthouse. I tilted and stretched my neck to see through the crowd.

The courthouse was truly the centerpiece of Bluebonnet Hills. It projected the same Victorian-inspired architecture, but on a more opulent scale. A central octagonal clock/bell tower jutted above a platform with four smaller, towered domes. The article I'd read in this morning's *Bluebonnet Bee* included its history, notably that it was built in 1896 and constructed from limestone, pink granite, and red and tan sandstone, all mined in Texas.

A woman, who I assumed to be Mayor Aviva Ernst, stood centered in the courthouse archway, flanked by four columns, two on each side of her. She wore a tailored pistachio-colored pantsuit that swished with her body as she moved. Her diamond jewelry—earrings, pendant, ring—reflected off the sunlight when she gestured to the crowd.

She said, "Our town's infamous fitness queen and owner of the Lonestar Gym, Barbara Lou Sinclair, will now deliver a few remarks about the health benefits of spending time around trees."

The smattering of polite applause suggested a definite disinterest in those benefits. As Barbara Lou ascended the courthouse steps, I noted her helmet hair and the two-sizes-too-small hunter green spandex bodysuit that she'd been poured into.

"Thanks, hon." She took the mic, as Aviva winced at being called "hon." Barbara Lou turned to the crowd. Her eyes were bulgy like a bullfrog. "The health benefits of trees take us back to the time of Johnny Appleseed …"

As Barbara Lou spoke, Aviva lifted a wine glass from behind a podium and slugged the contents. Guess I wasn't the only one getting Very Cherry Smashed.

Barbara Lou continued to ramble, and my professional interest in her speech was waning. I noticed a black Cadillac in the parking lot that had backed into its spot. Its windows were tinted dark, its headlights on, suggesting that the engine was running. The passenger-side door opened, and a teenage girl stepped out. She pulled her hoodie tight before disappearing into the trees. The headlights flashed, signaling a teenage boy, who jumped from behind a bush and into the passenger seat. Was this a drug deal? I strolled in the direction of the car, inspecting the grains of tree bark to appear casual.

About a minute later, the teenager jumped out of the Cadillac and shut the door. He pulled a ball cap down and then his eyes locked on mine. I busied myself with the bark, and when I looked again, he was gone. The Cadillac remained. Would a drug dealer drive such an expensive car? Wow, perhaps Jenny was right to call me a snob. I'm sure drug dealers appreciated a comfortable work environment too.

I set my drink down on the grass and reached inside my pocket, my fingertips brushing against my one remaining antidepressant. A few more would curb the withdrawal symptoms of the Zoloft, help manage the stress of seeing Jenny again. I was committed to the titration process, but the effects of the Very Cherry Smashed made the prospect of obtaining additional antidepressants quite alluring. Stop. What was I thinking? I was being reckless and dumb. But so what? Jenny quit school—twice—moved to Texas, bought a café. She wallowed in reckless and dumb and seemed overjoyed with the results. Why couldn't I? Perhaps knee-jerk decisions were inherited behaviors for the Tanaka siblings. I blamed genetics.

Before I knew it, I'd knocked on the driver-side window of

the Cadillac. The window rolled down about a third, and I stared into a pair of sunglasses.

Great, now what? What was appropriate drug-buying behavior? Chin up, shoulders back? Lips together, teeth apart? "Uh, hi." Brilliant opening. "Um, I . . . I saw you selling to those teenagers." I pointed behind me. "I need to buy some . . . stuff."

"Don't just blurt that out, cowboy." The window rolled down further. "Be cool, be cool." The driver flashed a gold tooth with his smile.

I swiveled my head around the parking lot, but everyone was facing the courthouse. "Sorry, I'm not familiar with drug etiquette. Cool was never my forte."

"Never your what?"

"Thank you for making my point."

"You a cop?" The dealer glanced at his rearview mirror.

"No, I just have anxiety."

"Get in." He cocked his head at the empty passenger seat.

That seemed dangerous, getting into a car with a stranger. "Could we do this out here?"

The dealer rolled up his window.

Fine. Probably not the time to recommend customer service training. I walked over to the car door and waited for it to unlock. I slid into the seat. The leather interior stunk like rank sneakers, and the back of my thigh rubbed against a piece of duct tape and . . . was that a cigarette burn or a bullet hole?

"What ya looking for?"

He stared straight ahead, and I noticed a deep scar that ran down the side of his face to his upper lip. I considered his question. I wanted Zoloft. Lots of it, 100 milligrams each. But low-dose antidepressants would do. Maybe a Xanax or two.

Or seven.

"Do you have any antidepressants?" I asked.

"I got Valium if ya want benzos. Or I got barbs."

"Barbs? You mean barbiturates? Those are serious Schedule II substances with significant potential for misuse and abuse."

"That a *no* on the barbs, cowboy?"

I picked at the duct tape. "Valium is hard on my stomach, and I had butter with my toast this morning. But maybe if I took half. How much?"

"Five for five."

I chewed the inside of my lip. "I don't know the lingo."

Scarface dropped his head, almost hitting the steering wheel. "Five dollars for five milligrams." He enunciated each word. "Twenty dollars total. Cash."

I did the math. "I don't need that many, so I'll take two for ten dollars, please. Unless you're running a special. Are there coupons?"

Scarface sucked air between his teeth and held his breath. "Five for five, cowboy. Twenty dollars, or get out of my car."

There would be no five-star rating for this customer experience. I reached for my wallet and dug out my debit card.

He glanced at the card with raised eyebrows. "Dude, cash only."

"This is practically cash. Don't you have one of those swipey things that connects to your phone?"

"Get out of my car."

"Seems like an essential item for a mobile entrepreneur."

"Now!"

"We can drive to the bank together if you insist." I reached for the seat belt but stopped when I felt something course and sticky.

Scarface lifted his T-shirt, revealing a gun. He tapped his fingers against it and flashed me a golden smile.

I pushed against the door. "Or, I could leave." My fingers fumbled for the handle, and I stepped backward out of the car. Before I could shut the door, Scarface popped the Cadillac into drive and inched out of the parking lot, disappearing down the street.

What was that? Reckless and dumb would require more practice if I adopted it as a new philosophy. I patted down my blazer, realizing I was still gripping my wallet. I slipped it into my inside pocket and turned.

There, parked two spaces away, was a Bluebonnet Hills police cruiser. Was it there the entire time? The officer's arm rested on the frame of his window, as if he'd been waiting for me.

Chapter 5

THE AVIATOR SUNGLASSES wrapped around the officer's face made it difficult to read his facial expression. Was he waiting for me to make a move? Thankfully, I didn't purchase the Vicodin. All I had in my pocket was the one legally prescribed antidepressant. I respected law enforcement, all authority really, yet lately I encountered them at my worst and my lowest. The temptation to turn and bolt wouldn't rehabilitate that image.

I sucked in a breath with the decision to let the situation play out. I stepped toward the cruiser, my arms outstretched, wrists facing up, ready for the cuffs and some swift Texas justice. But from a closer distance, I realized the officer was gazing in his rearview mirror, finger-combing his hair. Had he even noticed me? The arm he had propped outside his window was tanned, veiny and well muscled, and completely hairless.

"Howdy there, little man. Didn't see you there." The officer neglected his finger-combing long enough to flash me a mouthful of capped teeth. "Something I can do you for?"

I stared for a moment, realizing he hadn't noticed me with Scarface. My smile spread as the anxiety drained down my legs and pooled into the asphalt of the parking lot. I stumbled backward, grateful for the stay of execution. "Sorry, officer. My mistake."

"Chief, not officer," he said, though his focus returned to his hair. "You're not from here. New local or just visiting?"

I released a nervous laugh and then immediately covered my mouth. "Visiting. My sister runs the café."

He delivered another toothy grin. "Oh yeah, the Lotus Flower."

"Uh, you mean the café? It's the Cherry Blossom."

He adjusted the rearview mirror, satisfied with his coiffing efforts. "Guess I mix up my foreign flowers. Tanaka, right?"

I gulped. "Yes, Sho Tanaka. My sister's Jenny."

He popped the cruiser's door open and stepped down. He wore shorts, an uncharacteristic choice for a police officer, especially in April. His legs were also well defined, hairless, and the same shade of tan as his uniform. In fact, it was difficult to determine where the uniform ended and his skin began. Perhaps this optical illusion was a tactical defense.

"Tex Gunderson, chief of police."

I shook his outstretched hand, which resembled a catcher's mitt, and hinged my head back to look up. The guy was at least 6'3", 6'4" in height. His face was wrinkled around the mouth and eyes, perhaps from all the sun exposure needed to achieve that deep a tan. Still, for a man in his mid-forties, he was well preserved and in better shape than I had been at nineteen.

"Haven't had the privilege to break bread at your sister's café. Not a real fan of the Pad Thai." He slapped his stomach, suggesting Asian cuisine might interfere with his crunches.

The amplified voice of the mayor filtered from the courthouse and into the parking lot where we stood.

"And now it's time for our police commendation ceremony . . ."

Gunderson adjusted his shirt across the shoulders. "That's my cue. How do I look?"

"Uh . . ." I had nothing, so I gave a thumbs-up and tried the match the intensity of his smile.

Gunderson thanked me by making finger gun gestures, complete with *pow-pow* sound effects. "Welcome to Bluebonnet Hills, little man. My guys are here to protect and serve, but stay alert. We have a few thugs who prey on fresh meat. Catch you later." The hulking mass of hairless tan shot me another finger gun and ran to the courthouse.

I followed the noise of the cheering crowd, absorbing the chief's advice. Was that a pointed warning? Had he seen me with Scarface? If so, why didn't he intervene?

My original spot in front of the courthouse was taken; in fact, the crowd had almost doubled since I'd stepped away. Aviva remained on the top of the steps, a medal cupped in her palm. Next to her stood a uniformed police officer, one who wore pants. He stood at full attention, though he looked away from the mayor, suggesting a discomfort with public displays.

Aviva spoke into the mic. "Deputy Perkins, your impressive arrest of drug offenders has made everyone in Bluebonnet Hills sleep better . . ."

I glanced back at the parking lot. Deputy Perkins just missed the chance for a second commendation. Chief Gunderson had marched to the front, his chest puffed, his short-shorts barely longer than the arms he held to his sides.

Aviva passed the mic to an aide and pinned the medal on Perkins. More applause from the crowd. She then moved to the side, giving the deputy his moment. Perkins's pinched but appreciative smile suggested he would rather catch criminals.

"It's vital we recognize the superb work our police do." Aviva retook the mic and returned to center stage. "I wish our entire police force was full of honorable men such as Deputy Perkins. But it's not."

A few surprised groans came from the crowd. I caught Gunderson's expression, still toothy and bright, like the mayor had made a joke.

"Instead, this town's police force is rife with corruption. And it all starts at the top."

If the mayor's plan was to build suspense, she had been successful.

"The disappearance of our beloved mayor, my husband, left us numb and confused and heartbroken. But while we grieve, our chief of police watches this town fester and rot."

Gunderson's lips folded under his teeth, but he nodded at the crowd like everything was okay.

But Aviva wasn't stopping, and she clearly wasn't doing stand-up. "Drugs, poverty, assault, all on the rise and all being ignored by *him*. And when I ask questions, when I fight for you"—she stretched an arm to the crowd—"what does our chief do? He arrests *me*."

Aviva could whip her constituents into a fervor. There was a crescendo in crowd participation. Someone shouted, "Lock him up!" while another screamed, "Preach it, Aviva!" I looked for Jenny, who was a good distance away, managing her table, serving drinks, oblivious to this amazing sideshow. If this town needed revitalizing, it should promote these street performances and rename itself Dysfunction Junction.

Aviva ascended the courthouse steps with the discipline and fluidity of a ballerina. The effects of the light bouncing off her diamond jewelry only heightened the spectacle. "Chief Gunderson, you are a rogue officer. You falsely arrested me and then lied in the police report. You are a disgrace to this town and to your profession."

I scanned the crowd for Gunderson, who had disappeared. The volume of the crowd's murmurs increased, their heads swiveling back and forth to trade gossip and speculation.

Chapter 6

"Thought you might need a refill." Jenny appeared next to me with more Very Cherry Smashed. "How's it going here? I miss anything?"

"Everything." I took a greedy gulp of my drink and stared at the courthouse. A group of surprised-faced schoolkids were now performing a song about planting trees. Lots of jazz hands were involved.

"Oh?" Jenny asked. "You can tell me about it later. You okay hanging a bit longer?"

I lifted my cup to her. "Take your time."

"Uh ... thanks? I'll keep the booze flowing, too. Don't go hugging any trees."

The crowd had recovered from Aviva's confrontation, and their heads bopped along to the schoolkids' melody.

My cell phone dinged and then vibrated in my pocket. A notification from the Wild West Airlines app. I stepped away from the courthouse and swiped right for the update: "Lost in transit."

A wave of dizziness smacked me alongside the head, followed by a gut punch of nausea. The stress, the sun, and the booze were seeking their revenge. I wobbled sideways. My drink sloshed over the rim of the cup. I sucked the excess liquid off my knuckles, discovering that my hands were trembling. I fumbled to find my blazer pocket and pinched the antidepressant between my thumb and index finger.

I stumbled toward a tree for help with stability, but something caused me to trip. A brown, fluffy thing was in my path, and it streaked behind a tree. Was that a dog, or a giant squirrel? Whatever it was, it looked like a loaf of bread on four legs. I raised my palm to my mouth and saw the pill was gone. I lowered myself to the ground, setting down my drink and raking my fingers through the blades of grass.

"Don't walk away from me, Aviva," the male voice boomed.

I lifted my head in time to stand and sidestep the police chief and mayor.

Gunderson continued. "I thought we had an understanding, you and I. You perform your little political theater and play nice with the council, and I run the town."

He towered over her, but Aviva didn't appear intimidated. "But that *was* political theater. One of my better performances, in fact. Was that too impulsive for you? Apologies if my program change inconvenienced your bow-flexing." Her body swayed when she hefted her wineglass like a weapon.

Gunderson squinted, first at the wineglass and then at the

mayor. "Now, darlin', I think you've had a little too much to drink—"

"Don't call me darlin', you juiced-up frat boy." She glugged her wine. "And it's Arbor Day, everyone is drunk."

I'd drink to that.

"Just remember who's in charge," Aviva said. She lurched at the chief, a masterful fake-out that made him step back.

His chest rose, and he pointed his finger in her face. "You just remember who runs this town, *acting* mayor. Who keeps things in order, makes people feel safe. That ain't you. You mayors, y'all are replaceable. As you already know."

The slurping sound I'd made with my ice cubes broke the tension, but directed their attention to me. When channel-surfing, I had always flipped past the reality TV shows. Clearly, I'd been missing out.

Gunderson's jaw twitched. He smoothed his shirt and flashed me a smile. It was so genuine that it was unnerving. "You enjoying the festivities?" he asked me.

I attempted a reply, but sucked an ice cube down my throat instead. When I'd recovered, Gunderson gave me one last thin smile before stalking away, signaling his end to the confrontation.

Aviva, however, released a war cry and jumped on his back. She punched the meaty roll on his neck. Her other arm swung back, tossing the wineglass directly into my nose. I raised a hand to shield myself, dousing myself with Very Cherry Smashed. Ice-cold, sticky red liquid drenched my shirt and dribbled down my skin.

I tossed the plastic cup to the side and doubled over. Gunderson, the mayor still attached to his back, bucked backwards, his elbow jabbing me in the gut. I shot up for air, in time for one of Aviva's bracelets to fly off her wrist and smack against my cheek. I fell to my knees, tears streaming down my face.

Stay calm, stay calm. 1-2-3. 1-2-3. My nervous system would

eventually regroup, but my brain had other plans. I rolled on my back and closed my eyes, praying for air or death. Whichever came first.

"I haven't seen someone take a punch like that since my stage combat class," said the voice above me. "Of course, that punch was choreographed and completely fake. Are you faking?"

I opened my mouth to speak, but all that came out was a groan and some gurgles. I winced at the stinging sensation of a bag of ice cubes being pressed against my nose.

"How's the gut?"

I dragged my hand down my sticky and sore stomach. He tried to lift the bag of ice, but I held my grip.

"I don't think it's broken," he said. "The nose is pretty bendy, lots of soft tissue there."

"Pretty bendy?"

"Some people might call me a medical expert. I once had almost forty-five minutes of triage instruction for the show."

The show? I opened my eyes and blinked to adjust. He had a crooked smile and puffy rock-star lips. And he wore a black beret. Oh, no. No, it can't be. "Crazy mime! Crazy mime!" I attempted to stand, but my legs felt like cement blocks and pushed me down.

"In the episode, the one I learned triage for, my character posed as a genius tween neurosurgeon sent to stop a deranged diabetic candy striper from swapping patients' pudding with Greek yogurt . . ."

I felt his hand on my chest. Was he holding me hostage?

" . . . Anyway, in the climax, Nanny Sherbets, my very English nanny slash sidekick, lost her foot protecting me."

Did I have a concussion, too? "Lost her foot? Did she find it?"

His face fell. "Alas, a herd of cannibalistic wild boars nipped it off."

"Cannibalistic boars?"

"Season 2, episode 24, 'This Little Piggy Had Roast Beef.'"

The show? The show. That ridiculously named actor from that ridiculously named TV show. "Are you . . . are you Levi Blue?"

"*C'est moi.*"

My breaths grew shallow, fingers tingly, face clammy. I rolled over and teared at the grass blades. I needed that pill.

"What are you doing?" Levi asked. "What's happening?"

I pressed into any dirt clump that was roughly the same size. "Panic . . . panic attack. Need my anti—"

"Quick! Hug a tree!"

Hug a wha—? My body rose like a marionette. Levi had grabbed me from behind, opened my arms wide, and smooshed my cheek into the wounds of the bark.

"I saw this on TV, so it must be true. You should feel a sense of calm almost instantly. Are you calm yet?" He asked. "We also did an episode of the show where—"

I reached to grab his lips to silence him, but I missed. I snatched the beret, though, and then tossed it into the air.

"You're going into shock, bud." He thumped my cheek like it was a ripe cantaloupe. "Stay with me, bud."

I grabbed and gripped his hand. "Don't. Do. That."

"That's right, bud, squeeze my hand. Don't you die on me."

My knees buckled, loosening my grip around the tree. Cherry liquid dribbled down the corners of my mouth. My cheek scraped against the bark as I slipped further down the trunk.

Chapter 7

My limbs spasmed from the adrenaline surge that awoke me. I felt that momentary panic of not knowing where I was until I recognized the ceiling fan whirring cheerfully. I was in my bedroom, above the Cherry Blossom Café. How I got there, well, that was a mystery.

I stretched my arm to the *kusuri tansu*, groping for my phone, when the pain and the reminder of the Arbor Day Festival kicked in. I hissed in response to my throbbing abdomen, gingerly moving my hands over the cold, tender skin. My now fat lip was also tender, but I'd felt surprisingly little swelling. I'd dealt with these injuries enough with patients to predict there were no fractures.

As I pushed my hand back for my phone, my fingertips brushed a glass of cold water. I propped myself up by the elbows and turned to my side. The pressure in my head pulsed like a drill at the dentist. But I remained steady, breathing deeply through my nose until the dizziness passed.

It took a moment for the wetness of the water to penetrate through my dry mouth. I swished the water before letting it slide down my throat, which contracted a little. How long had I been asleep? No nightmares, none I could remember, anyway. I remembered a dog, but was that real or part of the dream?

I set the glass down after a second sip and attempted to turn. Levi Blue was asleep in a chair in the corner of my bedroom. I let out a strangled gurgle that soaked my bedding with water and forced Levi awake, his designer cowboy boots clomping onto the floor as he stood.

I had several questions for him, which I'd normally rattle off in rapid, snarky succession. For now, I started with, "How long was I asleep?"

"All night. Doc examined you on the square and then again last night. Said you mostly needed rest." Levi pushed up the sleeves of his preppy Western-style shirt. The solid teal cuffs were rolled over and offset the blue and gray plaid.

"Any prescriptions?"

Levi pointed at the *kusuri tansu.* "In the drawer."

I rolled to my side and paused at the fifteen different drawer options.

"Top row, far right," Levi said.

"Thanks." I pulled at the handle, sliding my body along the sheets to better reach the folded piece of paper inside. An anti-inflammatory, no pain pills. Drat. I propped against my pillows, closing my eyes at the temporary rush of dizziness. "How long have you been here?"

"About an hour. Your sister was here all night, but I volunteered to help this morning so she could open the café."

Wow. I must have given Jenny a scare.

Levi continued. "She also gave me permission to thump you again. No restrictions."

"That sounds like Jenny." I glanced down and realized I was wearing pink. I lifted the quilt up and yup, pink T-shirt and tiny pink shorts that were riding up on me and were covered in cartoon faces of a tween-age Levi Blue. I groaned, though not from the pain.

"That shirt's a collectible. And women's medium is a popular size."

I tilted my head to read the curly lettering on the T-shirt. It had that new, raw cotton smell. "What does it say?"

"*Trust Your Tween-stincts.* It was my catchphrase on the show; I said it every time I found a clue. Clever, huh?"

"It's certainly nuanced." My face flushed hot when I considered how I got into this ensemble. "You didn't, uh . . . have to dress me, did you?"

Levi shook his head. "Only contributed the wardrobe. Jenny explained your lost luggage situation, so I thought I'd help."

"Oh. Well, thank you. I appreciate that. Really." I scanned the bedroom but didn't see my blazer or pants. "Have you seen my actual clothes?"

"They were pretty stained after your Arbor Day stunt work. I suggested we pitch them, but Jenny said that would make the vein on the side of your forehead bulge." He leaned in and squinted. "I see what she means now. Anyway, I'm having them dry-cleaned, but I got you covered in the meantime."

Levi opened the wardrobe door and grabbed a hanger. He

revealed a long-sleeve plaid shirt, similar in style to his, but all I saw was more pink. Lots and lots of pink.

"Wow. That's . . . that's a shirt."

"It's salmon," Levi said, reading my facial expressions. "And there's some navy and green in the plaid. I think it upgrades that Edgar Allan Poe look you've been sporting around town."

"Edgar Allan . . . what does that mean?"

Levi scrunched his face. "Black blazer, black shirt, cream-ish pants with no clear cut or style? It's all sort of pale and tragic."

"Pale and tragic? *GQ* recommended those colors for my skin tone," I snapped. "And what's that thing hanging around the shirt collar?" I pointed to a thin black cord attached to a turquoise and silver stone. "Looks like a garrote. Is that the punishment for fashion crimes?"

"It's a bolo. You wear it like a tie. Seemed to complement your buttoned-up style." The corner of his mouth raised to a crooked smile. Levi returned the hanger to the wardrobe and then clapped his hands. "Now get dressed. Jenny's making us breakfast before we head out."

"Uh, us? Did you move in?"

"I'm staying at the B&B on the edge of town, but that's an excellent idea. Thanks for asking."

"I didn't—"

"Logistically, staying close makes sense since we'll be investigating as a team."

"What? Wait. What's happening?"

"This is why you're the brains of the operation. I'm just the looks, talent, and personality." He picked up an attaché case next to his chair and crossed to the door. "See you downstairs in five."

"Stop!" And he did. "I don't know what *this* is, but I'm not going anywhere with you. Certainly not to investigate . . . whatever you think needs investigating. I appreciate the unsolicited fashion advice, the change of clothes, and . . . the souvenir T-shirt, but I need sleep. Enjoy the rest of your visit."

Levi smiled. "Caustic wit with a crusty exterior. I bet you've been described as 'no-nonsense' and 'by the book.'"

I had, but I wasn't admitting it. "What's your point? What does that make you?"

"Carefree and unpredictable, of course. A loose cannon. But my shenanigans mask a vulnerability that only your sage sass can reach." He tapped two fingers against his heart. "It's what makes us a classic buddy comedy team."

I shook my head. Perhaps I had a concussion. "Sorry. You have me confused with another buddy. I left my rubber chicken in my pale and tragic pants."

"Oooh, I bet you have one heck of a tortured backstory. What is it? Wait, no spoilers." He rubbed his hands together. "I love dramatic third-act reveals. Why do you keep looking around?"

Cameras. There must be cameras hidden around here.

"All right, I get it. You're a pragmatist, that's your weakness. Let me convince you." Levi set the attaché case on the foot of the bed. It was a deep red leather with gold hardware and a large letter B monogrammed on the side. "Voilà." He pulled out a sheet of paper and waved it under my nose.

I blinked. "What's this?"

"The site plan for the *Tween of the Crime* fan museum. Construction should have been completed months ago."

I weighed my options. I didn't have the strength to leap up and run screaming from the bedroom. I also didn't have the self-confidence to do it in pink shorts.

Instead, I snatched the paper from Levi. Squares, rectangles, measurements, a map of the immediate area with a list of cross streets. The address, 1313 Mockingbird Lane, was printed in the corner. Yup, looked like a site plan to me.

I raised an eyebrow. "Is that all there is?"

Levi hefted a stack of papers from the attaché case and placed them in front of me. "And these are some invoices."

I fanned a few of the invoices on the bedspread. Based on the company logo, they all came from xyz Construction. Unimaginative business name, but everything looked official to me. For whatever that was worth. Each invoice included a line-item list of expenses with descriptions, rates, and quantities. My eyes bugged at the prices, but each invoice was stamped PAID in red ink. "I'm at a loss here," I said finally. "These invoices have all been paid in full, but you're saying the museum isn't finished yet? You should speak to the contractor."

"I can't."

"Why not? Isn't he local?"

"I can't find him. We were supposed to meet, but he never showed."

I glanced at the invoices as if they held better solutions. "If you can't find the contractor, move to the investors. See if they have any information."

"I don't think that will help us."

I sighed at the reference to *us*. "You don't know who's investing in your museum?"

"Of course. Me."

"Okay, and who else?"

"Who else do you need?"

"Hold on." I grabbed a few invoices and scanned the amounts. Three hundred dollars here, two thousand dollars there. "Are you saying *you* invested all this money?"

"It is my museum." When Levi plumped his lips he resembled a duckbill platypus.

I read the invoice descriptions again. "Why do you need so much lighting?"

"Atmosphere, obviously."

Obviously. Moving on, then. I pushed my face closer to read a description. "What's 'lost-wax casting'?"

Levi took the invoice from me, reviewed it, and handed it back. He cleared his throat. "That was for the statue."

Of course. For the statue. "What statue?"

"For the lobby."

I swallowed. "Did you commission a statue?" I looked at the next line on the invoice. "A *bronze* statue? Of what?"

"Of my tween likeness. Would aluminum have been better than bronze?"

"How much of this museum have you seen?"

"None. That's why I'm in Bluebonnet Hills." He plopped on the bed, crushing an invoice in his path. "The mayor convinced me how important the legacy of the show was to the town."

Hmm. I wondered how much convincing was needed, but I also remembered Aviva's Arbor Day performance on the courthouse steps. "She can be quite persuasive," I said.

"No, Fredrich Ernst, the real mayor. Aviva is the pretend mayor."

"Acting," I corrected.

"Precisely, she's acting like a mayor. Anyway, Fredrich said he'd manage the construction. That's how I connected with Javi. He and the mayor are childhood friends."

"Javi?" I asked. Where had I heard that name before?

Levi nodded, staring down at the floor. "The bronze bust was only one of the great ideas Javi pitched. We discussed an immersive media experience with clips from the show projected on the walls. A guided audio tour translated into thirteen languages—"

"Thirteen?"

"The show was very popular in Greenland. Some of our comedy actually translated better to Danish."

I didn't doubt it. "Levi, how much money have you invested?"

Levi counted on all his fingers. "Seven hundred and fifty."

"Thousand?!"

He pointed at the invoices. "Those are only a sampling."

I whistled, unable to imagine that amount of money. "I know you're a TV actor, but this is a lot of money. Where did you get it all?"

Levi shrugged, as if he'd never considered it. "Here and there. I go to conventions, and fans pay for autographed photos. I still get some royalties from the show, and then the second mortgage on my house in the Hollywood Hills. Well, it's my dad's house. He willed it to me after he died." His posture stooped, his shoulder fell.

"That sounds significant. When was your last acting job?"

His face brightened at the mention of acting. "Yesterday at the festival, of course."

"Paying job. Volunteer miming doesn't count. That should be illegal."

Levi's eyes drifted to the ceiling. "I guess it's been a while then."

"When's the last time you talked to Javi?"

"Last week, he sent me a text." Levi dug his phone from his jeans and scrolled with his fingers. He spun the phone and held it out for me to read.

"'I regret my terrible mustache. Need your platinum to give me courage.'" I pushed against my pillows. "Javi either has some unfortunate facial hair, or he needs an eye appointment."

"What do you mean?"

"*Terrible mustache.* That's a typo or some autocorrect. I'd guess he meant to write, 'I regret my terrible *mistake.*'"

Levi studied the phone. "Oh. That makes more sense." Then he smiled. "See? You're investigating already."

I blew out some air and avoided eye contact. "Look, I'm sorry this has all happened, but I can't help you. I'm only a visitor, and

Jenny is new to town. You're more familiar with these people than either of us."

"Please? You ask good questions and you're observant. You've got integrity."

I chuckled softly at that last part. "What makes you say that?"

"Yesterday, at the festival. You saw that guy in his car, selling drugs to kids, and you confronted him about it. I saw you."

My mouth fell open. "How did you . . .?" I balled the quilt and then launched into a coughing fit. I grabbed for the water, wincing in pain from the sudden movement. I took a few sips, composed myself, and stared into the almost empty glass. "I suppose you could visit the construction site. It's Saturday, so no one is probably working. Regardless, you could assess the progress for yourself."

Levi clutched his hands together. "And you'll go with me?"

I shook my head. "No."

Chapter 8

GETTING UP AND STRETCHING my stiff muscles felt good. After Levi left, I decided to dress and go downstairs for breakfast. Food and more water would help the healing process.

Levi's loaner shirt fit well enough. His preference for "slim fit" worked with my smaller frame, but the length made it difficult to tuck in. The pink plaid made me look like bruised cotton candy, but I was only wearing it downstairs and maybe later to the pharmacy. The black jeans blessedly muted my top half, though Levi was much taller than my 5'8", so I double-rolled the cuffs. The pant legs swung above my ankles like bell bottoms.

I grabbed the handrail as I slogged down each stair to the

café. When she saw me, Jenny erupted in laughter. I fake-limped to the lunch counter for sympathy.

Jenny made no effort to hide her amusement. "Sorry. It's just a unique look for you. Kind of like a busted-up rodeo clown."

"I bet you'd excel at jumping in and out of barrels," Levi said. He sat at the counter, surrounded by three plates of food.

I took the chair next to him, diverting my eyes as I'd just rejected his request for my help, only to change into the clothes he'd loaned to me.

"You're supposed to wear that untucked, like mine." Levi pulled the shirt out of my jeans as I tried to hoist myself into the swivel chair. "And where's the bolo?"

"It's a no-go on the bolo." I swiveled around to Jenny, who stood behind the counter.

She was still laughing but placed a mug of matcha and some ice water in front of me. "Levi was telling me about the new fan museum and dishing all the behind-the-scenes dirt on his show."

I sipped from my mug, letting the grassy sweetness of the matcha linger in my mouth. Jenny had whisked hot milk with the powder, enhancing its nutty flavor. "How long did your show air?"

"Sho's never seen *Tween of the Crime*." Jenny seemed to blame herself for my pop culture lapses.

"Five seasons." Levi spooned broken egg yolk over a piece of ham steak. "Ninety-seven episodes, plus the two-part Arbor Day special we filmed here."

"And don't forget the lost episode," Jenny added. "The one the censors won't even acknowledge exists."

Levi dropped his fork and smiled. Jenny had his full attention. "You know about that? You're a true TCI."

"TCI?" I asked.

"That's how my fans refer to themselves, of course. Tween Crime Investigators."

Of course.

"There are a lot of internet rumors about that lost episode," Jenny said. "No real information about what's in it or why it never aired."

"I still don't understand the objections." Levi shook his head. "The sequence in question was filmed very tastefully. Nanny Sherbets' eyebrows grew back eventually, and the sea lion never filed a formal complaint." He slouched in his chair and lifted a buttery toast triangle to his mouth. "Wish I could tell you more. But when the censors got involved, we all signed non-disclosure agreements."

"You signed an NDA over a sea lion?" I eyed the serving window for my breakfast.

"I don't know the legal jargon, something to do with habeas porpoise."

I set my mug down for a follow-up question when the line cook dinged a bell. Jenny retrieved and served me the plate.

"Poached egg with sourdough toast. Dry."

My eyes drifted from my plate to Levi's three, all heaped with breakfast delights: salty ham and bacon, buttery over-easy eggs and hash browns, fluffy pancakes with blackberry compote and real whipped cream. Was that ramekin filled with salmon, capers, and cherry tomatoes? "Why do I only get this?"

Levi wagged a strip of crispy bacon at me. "Because you're recovering, and you have a sensitive stomach."

"How did you . . .? Never mind." I sucked in the secondhand smoke from Levi's bacon.

Jenny refilled Levi's coffee cup from a carafe and nudged the ice water toward me. "What are you boys up to today?"

"Sleep."

"We're investigating a crime scene," Levi said.

"Interesting." Jenny raised an eyebrow and returned the carafe.

"There's been no crime." I pierced the egg yolk with my knife and let the velvety gold run into the crevasses of the toast. "And I'm not going anywhere with you. I told you that."

"Do you mind if I borrow your brother for some sleuthing?" Levi asked Jenny.

"Take my brother, please." She smiled at me. "I won't be too much fun today. The dishwasher stopped working this morning. Another repair for the never-ending list."

I'd forgotten to ask her for the café's financials. Perhaps I could review them from my bed, in between naps. I glanced at the saloon doors that separated the kitchen from the dining area. Both were hanging from their respective hinges. At least some repairs were getting done.

"I'd like to sit down with you later, review your expenses, food costs, savings, repair budget."

Jenny wiped her hands on her apron. "Sure, if you think you'd be interested in that. I have a pretty good handle on everything. Duncan's helped me there."

Duncan? I hadn't heard that name before.

"Who is this Duncan?" Apparently, Levi was curious too.

"I am this Duncan." A man's head popped above the serving window. "Jen, I replaced the water inlet valve on the dishwasher. I'm running it through a cycle now."

"Boys, this is Duncan Papadopoulos. *Reverend* Papadopoulos."

He looked to be in his early thirties, with tan skin and sandy brown hair. When he leaned in to shake my hand, I got a whiff of his cologne, something citrusy with a hint of wood smoke and spring rain. His hands were rough, like I was being gripped by a loofah sponge.

"Sho, it's nice to see you alert and moving this morning," he said.

"Duncan helped me get you up the stairs yesterday," Jenny said. "And then got you dressed." She said the last part with an impish grin.

I felt the blush on my cheeks. "Oh, you're the one who . . . ah, well, thanks."

"And I want to borrow that T-shirt sometime," Jenny added. "Never thought I'd be clothes swapping with my big brother."

My pink blush turned red.

"Sho, I hope the café gets your approval," Duncan said. "Jen's worked hard to make it a success. And it's a relief to no longer be the town newbie. Somebody else for people to haze."

Jenny laughed. Did she just bounce?

"Duncan moved to town a few months before I did," she said. "He's a great bookkeeper and has helped keep my ledgers straight."

"A preacher who knows math?" Levi sounded suspicious, though it was hard to detect the tone through all his food shoveling.

Duncan took a few steps back. "All part of managing a church. We're all running businesses here, so I help all my parishioners where I can."

Jenny giggled and touched his shoulder. Did she have a crush on Reverend Papadopoulos? Was that even allowed? She eventually noticed me watching her, the impish grin now plastered on my face.

"Eat your egg." She picked up a rag to wipe down tables.

"I have a question," Levi said, his mouth crammed with bacon. "How come you go by Jenny, and Sho, your name is more . . ." He chewed, literally, over his next word choice.

"More Japanese?" I offered. "Our parents gave us American first names and Japanese middle names. It connected us to both cultures, and then we decided which we preferred."

"I'm named after the host of a trashy talk show that my mother and Obachan watched," Jenny said. "My middle name is Sakura." She shuddered. "It means cherry blossom."

"Like the name of your café," Levi said. "You made the best of both names."

Jenny seemed to appreciate that take.

"What about you?" Levi turned to me.

"I prefer my middle name. As you already pointed out." I busied myself with the silverware, avoiding his tilted head and perked-up posture.

"Are you named after a talk show host, too?" He gasped. "Are you Geraldo Tanaka?"

"You're getting warmer," Jenny said, in a singsongy voice.

I rubbed the water spots off my butter knife. "My parents are big theater lovers, so that's what inspired them with me."

Levi almost levitated above his swivel chair. "Are you Merman Tanaka?"

The knife clanked when I dropped it on the counter. "It's Gilbert, alright? As in the composers Gilbert and Sullivan."

"Gilbert Tanaka." Levi chewed this over with more bacon.

"What about you?" Jenny asked Duncan. "Any embarrassing names in your closet?"

"Try being a kindergartener and learning to spell Papadopoulos," he said. "My parents are from Mexico and Greece, so the odds of me having any pronounceable names was low."

"Aww, c'mon." Jenny touched his shoulder.

He looked a little sheepish, but also appeared to enjoy the attention. "Like Sho, I also prefer my middle name. My first name is Yanni."

"That's not so bad," Jenny said. "I kind of like Yanni."

"Like that cheesy keyboardist with all the hair." Levi put down the bacon long enough to hold his arms out.

"Check, please?" I heard a café customer call to Jenny.

Jenny's body snapped to attention. She disposed of her rag and pulled an order pad from her apron pocket.

Duncan nabbed the order slip from her hand. "I'll take care of this, Jen." He returned her shoulder touch. "You stay and visit with your brother. I'll bus a few tables while I'm at it."

When he left, Jenny leaned in toward Levi. "So, what exactly are you investigating about your museum?"

"I suppose I'll start with your brother's suggestion of visiting the site, see what information I can dig up there." He sighed dramatically. "Course, that'll be a lot more difficult without a sidekick."

I ignored him and crunched my toast loudly.

"Have you talked to the mayor?" Jenny asked.

"Her office always says she's 'unavailable.' I tried to talk to her at the festival, but, well, the incident with your brother happened."

I wiped my mouth. "Were Aviva's accusations against Gunderson true? Did he falsely arrest her?"

"She was arrested for public intoxication," Levi said. "Gunderson found her sprawled in the middle of the street."

Jenny raised her index finger. "But she was in front of her house. Aviva claimed she was getting her mail and slipped on the wet street. She cited emotional anguish over her husband's disappearance. It makes sense to me. I think she's angry over how Gunderson is handling that investigation."

"What investigation?" Levi asked. "The beloved mayor vanishes one day. That's all they got. No leads, no nothing."

"This is the guy who gave up his US House seat to run for town mayor?" I asked.

Jenny ignored me and continued her gossip session with Levi. "You know why there's no investigation, right?"

"Spill it." Levi plopped his elbows on the counter.

Jenny turned and checked for small-town eavesdroppers. "Rumor is that Gunderson is launching a mayoral campaign against Aviva."

"No!" Levi made an explosion gesture with his hands. "Gunderson seems just bright enough to know he's not too bright. A poorly run investigation, especially one with a high-profile disappearing mayor, would be a negative for any campaign."

Jenny nodded. "He wants to stay scandal free."

"Teflon Tex."

I pushed my plate away. "If Aviva suspects corruption in the police department, why not just fire Gunderson? Seems like that would be a strong narrative for her to run on."

"Pretend mayors can't fire anyone." Levi said.

"He's partially right," Jenny said. "Police chief is an appointed position, and the town council is managing those appointments until we elect a permanent mayor."

Levi tapped me on the shoulder with a buttery toast triangle. "Maybe we solve the case of the disappearing mayor after we find my museum."

"I'm going to bed. Jenny, thanks for breakfast. Levi, thanks for the clothes." I moved to leave when a customer stepped next to my chair to address Jenny.

"Money's on the table, Jenny. Paid in cash again."

I'd forgotten to ask more follow-ups about this ridiculous seven percent cash discount. At least Jenny confirmed she had a system for tracking her money, or at least Duncan Papadopoulos did.

I started to say something when the line cook appeared at the kitchen serving window. "Jenny? Sink's leaking again. There's some water running. I really need this equipment to work. Orders are piling up."

"Be right there." She stabilized herself on the countertop. "And these repairs keep piling up. Javi said he'd have everything fixed before I closed on the café. I should have paid closer attention—"

"Javi?" I heard myself ask. "I remember now, you mentioned him last night. He's the one who used to run this place, and who runs most of the commercial real estate in Bluebonnet Hills?"

Jenny nodded. "Javi Zepeda."

I turned to Levi. "Is this also the Javi who's proposed these expensive ideas for your museum? The one you had a meeting with, but never showed?"

A loud crash disrupted my concentration.

"Sorry, sorry." Duncan kneeled on the rubber floor mats behind the lunch counter, picking up the hard plastic cups and silverware that had fallen when he dropped the bussing tote. "Doesn't look like I broke anything," he said to Jenny, who stood over him inspecting the mess. I swear she leaned over and sniffed him.

"I'll take care of this." Jenny bent over and picked up a fork. "Would you help in the kitchen? The sink's leaking again."

Duncan jumped up and disappeared through the saloon doors.

Something was off. Jenny bought the café under less than transparent circumstances, and Levi's museum problems confirmed these practices were synonymous with Javi Zepeda. If I could find Javi, perhaps I could understand what Jenny got herself into. "Levi, I'm going with you to the construction site."

"You are?" Jenny asked.

"Of course you are," Levi said.

Jenny winced. "Oh, I need my car this morning, in case I need to make a trip to the grocery store."

Levi waved his hands. "I'll take care of your brother. I already have our transportation ready out front."

Transportation? Levi Blue's use of the word sounded ominous. Was it too late to change my mind?

Chapter 9

"What's that?" The kid rode alongside me on his fire engine red bicycle, a thunderbolt sticker on his helmet. He was probably seven or eight years old.

I started to turn to him, but the contraption shook every time I gyrated. "A Segway." I adjusted the balance in my feet and gripped the handlebars of the two-wheeled death trap. Levi and I had scooted down a one-way street and wound down a residential area. Here, Bluebonnet Hills looked like Anytown, usA, with its single-family homes with manicured lawns and literal white picket fences.

"Does it go faster?" the kid asked.

"Probably. But I'm pretty risk adverse." I tapped my helmet, instantly regretting the sudden shift in movement.

"Is that why your face is beat up?"

I nodded. "I got punched by a drunken mayor, then again by an allegedly corrupt police chief. Now, I'm accompanying a delusional actor to his fan museum to help save my little sister from financial ruin."

"Maybe you can come to my house later to play army."

Levi, several hundred feet in front of me, took a quick right and disappeared from my sight. "The delusional actor would love that."

"Okay, bye." The kid pedaled away with such intensity that his feet blurred. He'd lap me if I didn't increase my speed.

I took the eventual right turn—a slow, wide turn—and wheezed toward the construction site. Sweat was already running down my cheeks. The newer road devolved into dirt and gravel, so I slowed even further to avoid a rock ricochet. Eventually, I maneuvered my Segway next to Levi's, standing straight to stop it. I relaxed my hands on the handlebars, stared straight ahead, and stepped down. When I met the hard ground, I silently celebrated not wiping out, which I had done earlier during Levi's demonstration.

"Why a Segway, of all things?" I asked. "And who has two sitting around?"

"As an Arbor Day icon, I shoulder many responsibilities. Green transportation is one of them."

"I guess it's not easy being green."

Levi's attention shifted from the site plan he held in his hands to the building in front of us.

The museum had been framed and wrapped in weather-resistant barrier. Stickers were affixed to the two front-facing windows and door, suggested they were newly installed. The museum was positioned off to the left of two additional structures. Their foundations were outlined by lumber and rebar frames, but some of the concrete had already been poured. I traced the ridges and grooves of tire tracks from the foundation to the road. The tracks were deep, filled with water and muddied from the rains, but the relative freshness suggested that foundations were poured recently. Several signs surrounded us. One was for XYZ Construction, and the other read, "DANGER. CONSTRUCTION SITE. UNAUTHORIZED PERSONS KEEP OUT."

"This is not where I thought it was." Levi studied the site plan again. "There's nothing here. The proximity to the square is awful. It's not what Javi told me. Something's not right."

It was oddly quiet, with no traffic sounds and only the occasional chirping of birds. It made me think of those movies where a bunch of teenagers go to a remote area for a Halloween party and get murdered by a maniac.

"Where is everyone?" Levi asked. "Lunch?"

"We just ate breakfast, and I told you, it's Saturday. I pointed to the three orange portable toilets next to the museum. "But someone comes here."

The rocks and dirt crunched under Levi's boots. "Let's take a closer look. Careful of the ground, there are still some soft patches from the rain."

"The sign says, 'Unauthorized Persons Keep Out.'"

"It's my museum, I'd say I'm authorized." His chin lifted, and then he broke into a smile. "Tanaka, look. There's that dog."

On the top step of the building sat a small dog, blinking at us. It had a sturdy, thickset frame, a smooth reddish-brown coat, and a flat face. Its black muzzle and whiskers looked like it had a beard. The loaf of bread on four legs from yesterday.

I sighed relief. "Good, you see it too."

"She's been following me since I arrived in town. At first, I thought it was because I carried bacon in my pocket. But she might have a message for me."

"Bacon in your . . .? Never mind." I centered the dog in the frame of my phone camera and snapped a photo.

"What are you doing?"

"I'll upload this photo to the local neighborhood app. Someone might know where it lives. In the meantime . . ." I ran the photo through an object ID app. "Our little bearded friend looks to be a Brussels griffon."

"Her eyes are very expressive; she knows stuff. And who couldn't love that cute, li'l smooshy face?" He squatted and held his hand out. "Come here, sweet baby."

"How do you know it's a she?"

"She follows me around and can't take her eyes off me."

Hmm. I read more background from my phone. "Apparently they were originally bred to be rat dogs on ships." I glanced up and saw the dog nudge the door open and disappear.

"Let's go rat hunting then." Levi pointed to my helmet. "You can take that off now."

"There are roughly 150,000 injuries on construction sites per year." I knocked twice on the hard plastic. "This stays on."

Levi climbed the two steps to the building. I followed. The smell of funky body odor and rotting food was unbearable. I bonked my nose when I raised my hand to shield it. My eyes pooled with water, but the pain distracted me from vomiting. Levi unhooked a button on his shirt to better pull the fabric up and over his nose.

I stood in the doorway, adjusting to the low lighting. The room was divided into two, the connecting wall covered in drywall. Drywall also hung over both the windows, strangling any natural light from shining through. Someone had at least cut the excess drywall around the door frame. The floors were concrete slabs, but were otherwise bare.

There were some clumps of mud and dirt leading into the smaller of the two rooms, but no other evidence of any construction work. No tables or saws, no hammers or nails, certainly no bronze bust of Levi Blue. The outside had been bare too; no dumpsters or equipment or debris of freshly cut lumber. Only the portable toilets, which now seemed out of place in absence of everything else. I glanced at Levi, and the disappointment on his face confirmed we shared similar thoughts.

He sighed. "Maybe it'll come together in the end. It happened this way on my show. Everything seemed unfinished and then it all magically came together."

"That was less magic and more a full-time production crew."

"Haven't you watched those home renovation shows? Everything gets done at the last minute, usually in fast motion and to a jaunty musical number."

Couldn't argue with that logic. Instead, I squinted into the darkness of the smaller room. Was something moving in there? I activated the flashlight app on my phone. Stepping carefully into the darkness, the stench became more potent. I stopped, swiping the phone in a horizontal direction. There was a back door along the wall, perhaps where the dumpster and equipment shed were.

I noticed several shapeless mounds on the floor, in the corner. I wanted to step further, but the stench would have flattened me. I held the phone out as far as my arm stretched, noticing a pile of colorful knitted blankets. Afghans, I believe they were called. Their vibrant colors—minty blue, tangerine and goldenrod, cotton candy pink—matched my shirt and contrasted with the minimalist and depressing decor. I swear the mound wiggled. I breathed to steady my arm and blinked to let my eyes readjust. No, I was seeing things. These dizzy spells were getting worse. I should have stayed at the café and napped.

I whisked the flashlight against the wall to a black plastic trash bag overfilled with empty food cans and dark glass bottles. If there was a dumpster, it wasn't being used.

"Tanaka, over here," Levi called from the other room.

I walked toward fresher air. "Someone's been here," I said. "Sleeping here, anyway."

Levi scratched his head. "Open the door, get some more light in here. I want you to see something."

I complied. Levi squatted near the wall, running his hand over an area of drywall. "Part of the wall was cut away and put back."

I bent at my knees, pushing up the bike helmet that slipped over my forehead. There was a jagged wall chunk secured with clear packing tape. "Aren't those imperfections of the process? Don't you spackle over drywall?"

"This corner is bulging, something's poking out." Levi flicked the corner of the tape, eventually grabbing a big enough piece to tug at.

"What are you doing?"

Levi continued to tear the tape, the cutout drywall bulging further from the wall. He rose on his knees, gripped the bulging corner, and pulled, sending a cloud of dust through the room. The drywall eventually splintered and knocked Levi back. Undeterred, he reached his arm into the hole, grunting and straining, and removed a large plastic bag. "No rat yet, but we discovered some buried treasure."

Holy . . . I backed into the open door. "Is that . . .?"

Levi dropped the bag and several stacks of money fell out. "Money, money, money." He flopped down and paged through a stack. "These are all ones." He flipped through a second stack. "This one's all fives."

I looked down and George Washington stared back. "These all appear to be small denominations. How much is there?"

Levi removed the band of a stack and was organizing the money into piles of ones, fives, and tens. "Hard to tell. Each stack has a unique combination of bills. But there's thousands here, at least." He shot me a lopsided grin. "Don't you just want to roll in it?"

I wrinkled my nose. "Paper money can carry more germs than a household toilet. The flu virus can live on a single bill for over two weeks."

"You even overthink *dirty* money." Levi groaned when he stood, stretching his long arms into the air. "There's another bag in there. I'm going to—"

"Shhh, listen. Do you hear that?" I heard a scratching from the smaller room. I tilted my ear in that direction.

We both froze, listening.

"Probably the dog." Levi's arm was already back in the hole.

I peeked around the wall where the scratching sound was louder. I redirected my phone/flashlight and stepped into the blackness.

Zeroing in on the scratching, I flicked the light across the floor. There was movement under the mound of colorfully crocheted afghans, and, suddenly, the mound rose to my eye-level and lunged at me.

I screamed. It screamed. It was the most colorful ghost I'd ever seen. Actually, it was the only ghost I'd ever seen.

A second colorful mound rose next to the first one, this one even taller. It grabbed my shoulder, causing me to drop the phone. The light from the camera lens blinded me. I stumbled back and blinked away the spots and floaties. When I recovered from the shock, I released a high-pitched scream that would make little girls proud.

"Run for your life!" I bolted out the door, leaping over both steps, and landed on the mushy outside ground. I pushed my body up with my hands, ignoring the pain pulsating through my body, and continued to run toward the street.

I almost smacked into Deputy Perkins, the officer who was commended at the festival. He leaned against the police cruiser, resembling a stuffed grizzly at the entrance of a sporting goods store.

"I'm . . . I'm so glad to see you." I doubled over and gasped for air. My most recent encounters with law enforcement had not been overly positive, but I could change that now. "We were in there, and ghosts . . . spooky, colorful . . ." I wiggled my fingers and made a *boo* sound.

Perkins stood still, his arms crossed. "You alone, son?"

I sucked in a breath. "No, I'm . . . I'm here with Levi Blue."

"Levi?"

I raised my hands to my mouth. "You don't know Levi Blue? The actor? The star of *Tween of the Crime*?" Whoa, wait a second. Did I just say that?

"I know Levi," Perkins said. "But I don't see him with you."

I turned to the building. The door remained open, but no sign of Levi. "I thought he was right behind me. Maybe . . . maybe he was eaten?"

"Eaten? By the spooky, colorful ghosts?" Perkins removed his sunglasses. "Son, I'm just going to ask flat-out. Are you high?"

"Not at the moment." The words tumbled out before I could finesse them. "I mean, I used to take Zoloft, but that doesn't make you high. Though I've read studies . . . addicts will crush a bunch up and then snort it. But not me, I just take them orally." My brain shouted *shut up*, yet my mouth wouldn't listen. "I'm prescribed the Zoloft, I'm not taking anything illegal. I bought *nothing* from Scarface, and *not* just because he kicked me out of his car." I flashed the scout's-honor sign. "So . . . nothing to bust here. Well, my nose, but that's already busted." I released a bark of laughter and then covered my mouth.

A beat later, Perkins said, "Son, I'm going to need to see that prescription."

I dug into my pocket for the prescription from the town doctor and handed it to Perkins. "This one's not for an antidepressant. It's the anti-inflammatory the doctor prescribed after my accident at the festival."

The deputy studied the paper and then me. "You're Jenny's brother, the one from yesterday. Shoe?"

"Sho."

He nodded. "Shoe Sho, sorry."

"Good morning, deputy." Levi approached from behind, the dirt crunching under his boots. "We were looking for a stray dog. She darted in there, but we can't find her. Sho, you dropped your phone." He handed it back to me. I saw a missed text from Jenny, but I'd read that later.

"Where have you been?" I asked Levi from the side of my mouth.

"Uttingpay ethay oneymay ackbay inyay ethay allway," Levi said.

"What?"

"Putting the money back in the wall," Perkins translated. "Pig Latin, right, Mr. Blue?"

"I didn't know you were bilingual!"

"What money?" Perkins didn't miss a beat.

I began, "The money we—"

"—the money we're using for the dog," Levi said. "We're offering a reward for any information on her. Sho took a picture. Show him the picture, Sho." Levi bumped my elbow with his. I reached into my pocket, but Perkins waved his hand.

"No need. Mr. Blue, this is the construction site for your museum. Far as I'm concerned, you're free to poke around."

"I am? I mean, I am. Thank you, deputy. You don't know where we could find Javi Zepeda, do you?"

Perkins shrugged. "At home? It's Saturday."

"Have you seen him recently? Javi?" I asked.

He scratched his chin and his eyes drifted toward the construction site. "Not for a few weeks, probably. Why?"

Levi stepped almost in front of me. "Our wires must be crossed. We keep missing each other."

Perkins studied Levi and then put his sunglasses back on. "Uh-huh. Well, I'm just checking everything out." He retrieved a small notepad from his back pocket and popped it open with a wrist flick. "Barbara Lou Sinclair reported some suspicious-looking characters casing the neighborhood on space-age contraptions." He pointed the pad at the Segways. "Those yours?"

"Suspicious looking?" I stomped my foot. "The woman with helmet hair and bug eyes called us suspicious looking?"

Perkins's head skimmed from my helmet to my shirt to my jeans. I folded my arms to mute the pink plaid.

"Don't pay Barbara Lou any mind." He popped the door of his cruiser. "Folks are just a tad jumpy. We've had a few break-ins and some encounters with the homeless. Bit out of the ordinary for Bluebonnet Hills."

"Is that who's living in there? Homeless?" I pointed to the construction site.

Perkins twitched. "You mean your spooky, colorful ghosts?"

"Yes." I glanced to Levi. "Er, perhaps? I don't know."

"You'll have to excuse my friend, deputy. He's had a lot of excitement, what with the festival and the new wardrobe. Probably best I get him home for a nap."

Perkins nodded and stepped into the cruiser. "You be careful out here, Mr. Blue. And good to meet you, Shoe Sho." He started the car and grabbed a radio receiver.

When I saw the taillights of the cruiser disappear, I turned and glared at Levi.

Chapter 10

THE ONLINE WHITE PAGES returned twenty-four records for the name "Javi Zepeda" in the Austin area. Thankfully, only one had an address in Bluebonnet Hills. Besides that Javi was in his fifties, all we learned from the record was that Javi was a nickname for Xavier.

I glanced at the numbers on the mailbox, confirming the address. "And stop telling me to *chill*," I said to Levi.

We'd been bickering about the encounter with Deputy Perkins and the wall of money since we got off the Segways. My missed text from Jenny was a request for me to pick up the new centerpieces for the café. As soon as I'd spoken to Javi, I'd visit the florist, and then home for a nap, and that would be the end of these shenanigans with Levi.

Levi blew air from his lips. "I just suggested you relax. You didn't lie to Perkins. You spilled your guts; tried to, anyway."

"I don't lie," I repeated my mantra.

"That's why you have me to help, all part of our dynamic. Besides, no one gets into madcap adventures by telling the truth."

I shook my phone at him. "This is fun for you? We're not in a sitcom, doing spit takes and pratfalls. There are bags of cash in that wall, which we didn't inform the police about. That makes us look suspicious. There's a reason I don't do madcap."

Levi pointed at the bike helmet I still wore but had enough sense to zip his distinctive lips. I unsnapped the strap and tossed the helmet at the parked Segway.

If it had been placed anywhere else, Javi's house would look like any old, nondescript home. The white siding gave the boxy exterior some dimension, the pumpkin-colored front door and window shutters a pop of color. But all this ordinariness was beautifully framed among a grove of pecan trees that stretched through the backyard and beyond. The sprawling grove gave the entire house a mystical element, like we were approaching a cottage in an enchanted forest. My internet research found the home had been built in 1926, but I suspected those trees had stood there long before.

I took the single step onto the porch and searched for the doorbell, finding none. I knocked. "I'll let you take the lead here," I said to Levi. "Then I'll ask some follow-ups about the café."

Silence.

I turned my head. Where did he go?

Footsteps approached from the other side of the door. Now what? Were there still encyclopedia salesmen? I wasn't a believable paperboy, but in this outfit, I could pass as the ice cream man.

The latch clicked when the door unlocked. Searching for a plan, I puffed my cheeks . . . and then blew the air out into Levi's face.

"How did you get in?"

Levi stood inside the house, flashing a grin. "All in the training. In one episode of the show, I entrapped an agoraphobic cat burglar. I learned all kinds of tricks."

Agoraphobic cat burglar? I had questions about those logistics.

"There's a side door on the garage. It was unlocked." Levi opened the door wider, a further invitation to break and enter. "No one's here."

The living room looked minimalist. A couch. A recliner pointed at a flat-screen TV. A standing fan pointed at the recliner. I noticed the twirling blades of a ceiling fan, seemingly a Texas-home fixture.

Levi flipped through a stack of mail from the side table. "I'll stay out here and check the kitchen. You search the bedrooms."

I glanced at the open kitchen. Dishes were drying on a towel. If we were alone, it hadn't been for long. "Five minutes, then I'm leaving." I headed to a hallway that led to the bedrooms. "What am I looking for?"

"Clues," he said, as if I'd just asked the color of the sky.

The master bedroom was small, but it had two large windows that showcased the backyard: a lush green lawn and the pecan trees that ran the fence line. Even parts of the deck were built around the trunks. Javi certainly preferred his décor simple and white—white walls, white curtains, white bedspread with two black decorative pillows.

Beside the bed, the white four-drawer dresser was the only piece of furniture. I rested my hand on the knob of the top drawer and stopped. I wouldn't violate his privacy like that; my questions wouldn't be answered with the contents of a dresser drawer.

My nose tickled, and I snorted to shake the scent tickling my nose hair rather than rubbing it away and risking more pain.

I followed the scent to the connecting bathroom, which was bathed in natural light. Various choruses of Texas songbirds chirped through a window, which was hinged on the top and opened at the bottom for ventilation.

The tickle in my tender nose intensified alongside the urge to rub it. I traced the offending irritant to a bottle of body wash that I grabbed from the shower caddy. The bottle's label assured me that Canyon Creek's citrus wood body wash was an all-in-one purifier with moisture-locking properties. I'd smelled it before, I noted as I set the bottle down. Water droplets set in the shower pan, indicating someone had been here recently. My head started to thump; we needed to leave.

I quickly scanned the bathroom and zeroed in on the medicine cabinet. I opened the mirrored door to a cornucopia of drug bottles. Painkillers, strong ones, with codeine, morphine, and oxycodone.

"Oh, my." I stared at a bottle of antidepressants. My hand was already moving toward it, but I clamped my fist shut and pulled back. Get it together, Tanaka. I couldn't do this. Could I? I peeked into the bedroom, confirming I was still alone. Before I second-guessed it, I grabbed the bottle. It felt empty. I shook it, no rattle. I twisted off the cap to confirm. Empty.

I shook the bottles of painkillers, one by one by one. Empty. Empty. Empty. The bottles had all been prescribed to Javi, but the print on some of the labels was worn or torn, and I couldn't locate the prescriber's name.

The nose tickling was approaching the climax: a sneeze was coming. Carefully, I raised my upper arm to use as my human sneeze guard. The intensity of the sneeze echoed off the walls. I winced at the pain pricks around my nose and mouth.

"You back already, brah?" I heard someone ask.

I froze. The voice had traveled through the window.

I took two baby steps backward and then raised up on my

tiptoes to see over the frosted window pane and into the backyard. Scarface, the drug dealer from the festival, sat with his back to me, drinking coffee, reading from his phone. Leaving the medicine cabinet open, I padded into the living room.

"Check these out." Levi held up a postcard in one hand. He waggled the fingers of his other hand, displaying a black plastic contraption pinched on his fingertip.

"Scarface is here. He's drinking coffee on the patio."

"Al Pacino is drinking coffee on the patio?"

"What? No. We need to leave now." I squinted at the contraption on Levi's finger. "Where did you find that?"

"Next to the recliner. What is it?"

"An oximeter." I grabbed the postcard. The image on the front was a sepia-toned photo of San Francisco's Golden Gate Bridge.

"Javi sent it."

"Put that back." I pointed at the oximeter. I started to turn the postcard over when the scraping sound of a chair on concrete came from outside. Scarface needed his coffee refilled.

I dropped the postcard and headed to the door while Levi attempted a layup to return the oximeter to its original spot.

I bolted out of the house and zigzagged toward the nearest pecan tree. Levi quickly shut the door behind him and pressed himself against the exterior of the house. He held a finger out, signaling me to wait. I braced against the trunk and breathed.

1-2-3. 1-2-3. 1-2-3.

Levi dashed to the other side of the tree, his face flushed. "That was—"

The door to Javi's house flew open. Levi pumped his arms as he jogged backward to another tree. I stuck my head around the trunk and saw Scarface. He yelled inaudibly into his phone, his head craned down the opposite side of the street.

1-2-3. 1-2-3. 1-2-3.

A numbness settled into my lower body. The front door finally shut, but I propped myself against the tree, concentrating on the cheeps and chirps of birds. Levi surprised me from behind, but I felt too numb to jump.

"You . . . okay?" He tried to catch his breath.

I nodded, and the movement replaced some of the numbness with a tingle. I moved my fingers and toes and allowed the tingle to sting my body into recovery. "No . . . No more of that," I said, though my voice sounded disconnected. I patted my body to ensure I was in one piece. I felt a bulge in the back pocket, realizing I still had Javi's empty prescription bottle.

Chapter 11

I FOLLOWED LEVI ON THE SEGWAY, down the same residential street from before. The familiar setting helped settle my nerves from the near-miss encounter with Scarface. I breathed in the sweet scent of cut grass and enjoyed the damp air on my face. Rain was coming, reminding me of Seattle.

But Levi's speed increased, and the cookie-cutter homes with the white picket fences disappeared. My suburban stress release turned into an unfamiliar two-lane street surrounded by massive trees that bowed to us. We were lost. The tree lines eventually disappeared, opening to larger homes built on larger lots. Levi's Segway leaned left, and he parked beside a circular drive.

I pulled alongside him. "We passed the square. Let me pull up the directions on my phone."

"No need. This is where I meant to go."

I stared up the mammoth drive, which led to about twenty stone steps, which led to a front door the same height as a two-story McMansion. "I'm making the bold prediction that *this* is not the florist. Our next planned stop."

"*Your* next planned stop. Plans hurt my head. This is just a quick pit stop."

"Where are we?"

"The mayor's house. You want to find Javi, you want answers about the café, maybe she can help."

I wanted to argue, but my throat was already hoarse from my earlier protests. Instead, I took off my helmet and stepped off the Segway. I thought about kicking it to register my mood, but I'd probably break a toe.

"Isn't it amazing?" Levi asked as we began the incline up the drive.

"Uh, it's big, a little gaudy. There's six different styles of windows on the front alone." We passed a line of topiaries, all pruned to draw the eye up and to the mayor's house.

Levi stopped halfway up the drive to take in the view. "The house sits on over nine acres and backs up to the Guadalupe River." He gave my shoulder a swat. "Rafting, kayaking, floating the river, that's how this town should revitalize itself. There's an opportunity that isn't being monetized."

I responded with a noncommittal nod and shrug.

He continued. "We did a lot of exterior shots here for *Tween of the Crime*." Levi pointed at a nearby oak. "That's where the swarm of killer bees chased me up a tree."

Lucky bees. Eventually, we'd trekked up the steps to a large glass door trimmed in dark wood. The doorbell chimed like Big Ben. "How do you want to play this?" I asked Levi. "Let's avoid the wall money, I . . ." I glanced at the empty space beside me. I was talking to myself.

Levi tap-danced up and down the stairs, counting the beats out loud. I pictured him in a movie musical, tapping on the rooftops of London.

He stopped and smiled at the sense memory. "I began my Act Two dance here and then tapped down to the chicken processing plant."

Aviva answered the door with bloodshot eyes, wearing a burgundy robe. I breathed in a faint herbal scent like lavender, mixed with the pungent fruitiness of wine. Her glazed expression drifted to Levi, who flap-step-stomped behind me.

"Good morning, Madam Mayor." Nothing to see here, folks.

Aviva continued to stare, blinking wildly, as if her brain short-circuited from the image processing. The clickety clack of Levi's boots ceased, and he slid beside me.

"*And save some gizzards fer me,*" Levi sang, no doubt a lyric from the song that accompanied his dance.

Aviva shook her head, signally she'd rebooted. She delivered a relaxed smile. "Of course, they shot some of your little show here. Please reminisce, but don't linger too long. I have nosy neighbors." She moved to close the door on us.

"I'd love to meet the neighbors, but we're here to discuss your unfortunate treatment of my good buddy Sho here."

I stiffened and stared at Levi. How'd I get involved with this?

Aviva fingered the rope of her robe. She studied my face with an expression that toggled between curiosity and revulsion. I turned away, self-conscious from the scrutiny.

"I suppose I should apologize for my behavior yesterday, Mr. Tanaka," she said finally. "And for doing . . . that to you. Are you sure that was all me?"

Should apologize? I hadn't come for an apology, but Aviva's lack of sincerity was irksome.

"There's a chance you broke his nose," Levi said. "We're actually on our way to Austin for some x-rays and a consultation with a world-class rhinologist."

I turned away again, this time to roll my eyes.

Aviva rubbed the knots in her neck. "Of course, I'll pay for any medical expenses. I will need documentation, though, that treatment is related to the alleged incident."

Alleged incident? She'd lost my vote. I cleared my throat. "We also visited the construction site, to check the progress of Levi's fan museum."

"Wonderful." Aviva clasped her hands and held my stare. I couldn't tell if she was clueless, or just that good.

"Unfortunately, there wasn't much progress to assess."

"Is Javi behind schedule?" She laughed. "I'll review his progress reports next week and get back to you. Thank you for the personal update." She moved to close the door again.

"We were hoping you'd have the personal update," Levi said. "You know, before Sho gets his x-rays."

Aviva pursed her lips to trap her reply. "All that sounds delightful, Mr. Blue. If you call my office on Monday, I will . . ." Her gaze drifted past us; her face froze. Before I could turn, she made a sweeping gesture and stepped away from the door. "Do come in. VIPs of Bluebonnet Hills needn't make an appointment."

We stepped into a foyer big enough to play a game of tennis, sunlight streaming through all six types of windows. But the natural light was too yellow to give the foyer any warmth.

Curiosity at what Aviva saw caused me to turn and look. A green hatchback circled the drive, rattling and shaking as it hit the street and sped off.

Jenny? Why would she be out? I grabbed my phone and texted her: *Where are you?*

Aviva pushed against the shut door. She, too, pulled a phone from her robe. "Excuse me, gentleman." The typewriter sound effect echoed through the foyer as she composed a text. I looked down at my screen to see Jenny responded to my question with an eye roll emoji.

"Who was that?" Levi had noticed the hatchback. Did he also suspect Jenny?

Aviva gave a noncommittal shrug and crossed to a hallway. "I was making coffee. We'll be more comfortable in the kitchen."

She led us into an open kitchen outfitted with marble countertops, stainless steel appliances, and a sea of natural light that still failed to give me any warm fuzzies. Aviva passed me a basket heaped with assorted K-cups and tea bags.

I selected a green tea bag. Levi reached over my shoulder and plucked a hot chocolate K-cup. "We noticed the sign for Javi's construction company outside the museum. Does he manage all the projects in Bluebonnet Hills?"

The coffee maker spat the last of Aviva's drink into her cup. She added a massive amount of sugar to it, clanking the spoon as she stirred. "He's a key player in the town's revitalization. The state requires us to solicit bids for every project from women and minority-owned businesses. Javi always underbids because he loves this town." She walked over to the kitchen table. "I'm sure your sister has mentioned all the help Javi has given her, securing that small-business grant for her renovations."

A record screeched in my head. What grant? Jenny never mentioned grant money. Based on my observations, the café appeared to be in disrepair, and Duncan Papadopoulos was the resident handyman. Was Jenny paying Duncan, or was she saving that money for something else? I lifted the lever of the coffee machine, removed Aviva's used cup, and pressed the button for hot water.

"Do you have any peppermint syrup? For my cocoa?" Leave it to Levi to always have food on the brain.

Aviva pointed at the pantry with her spoon. "There might be some peppermint schnapps in there, left over from the holidays."

As my cup filled with hot water, I searched for a trashcan to dispose of Aviva's used K-cup. I followed a trail of red wine dribbles to a pull-out cabinet. Unsurprisingly, the trash can was empty except for two empty wine bottles. I recalled our conversation at breakfast about Chief Gunderson arresting Aviva for public intoxication. I took a seat across from Aviva, toying with the string of my tea bag, contemplating how to casually ask about the grant money.

Aviva leaned across the table, her gaze locked on the pantry. "I'm afraid that little fan museum is a low priority. It wasn't part of our master revitalization plan."

I snorted. "The public isn't clamoring for a behind-the-scenes look at the psychedelic cow tipping dream sequence at the Red Poppy Corral?" It was a cruel comment that I instantly regretted.

"You're terrible!" She grabbed a napkin and dabbed the sugar-coated coffee she'd spat out from her mouth. "But Levi's self-funding that museum, and, well, he's delinquent on payments. Javi is only managing the construction as a favor, so I suspect that explains the lack of progress."

The invoices Levi produced this morning didn't show he owed money. In fact, the amounts he'd paid seemed like enough for five museums. Still, he'd mentioned the various funding sources he'd pieced together, including a second mortgage on his home. Perhaps Levi's desire to be immortalized in bronze was pushing him into debt.

"Found it." Levi popped out of the pantry and flashed the bottle of schnapps.

"I understand Javi's a family friend," I said to Aviva. "Your husband connected him with Levi for the museum construction."

Aviva straightened in her chair. "They grew up together. Fredrich was born here, his family's been here since its founding.

Javi's family immigrated from Mexico when he was a baby. Legally, of course." Her voice emphasized that last point. "I didn't know Fredrich then, but they must have been opposite ends of the spectrum. My Freddy, sweet and shy, focused on school. Javi was . . . he was wild. He wanted to tear apart the world and rebuild it from the ground up. Literally."

I nodded. "He has a passion for construction?"

"He can fix anything. Javi tells stories about working on construction sites as a minor. Supervisors took advantage of him and paid what they wanted. But he loves the work."

Levi set his mug of peppermint hot chocolate next to me. "Do you have any reason to believe he's missing?" he asked Aviva.

I sipped my tea. Levi's question didn't defy logic; Fredrich Ernst had presumably disappeared, so Javi could also be missing. Perhaps the two were together. But what was their connection? Fredrich ran for mayor to bring prosperity back to his hometown, and Javi was the point person for the entire revitalization. Did they make enemies, get in someone's way? And what was Scarface doing in Javi's house? How did he connect to all of this?

"Has someone reported Javi missing?" Aviva asked. "Wasn't he at the festival?"

"I didn't see him," Levi said.

It occurred to me I only knew Javi by reputation. I might have passed him several times yesterday and not known it.

Aviva tugged at her robe. "The disappearance of my husband has been torturous. Two disappearances might finish me." She blinked as if to keep the tears at bay. "And if this becomes a pattern . . . I fear I'm the next target."

We sat in silence, unsure of an appropriate follow-up.

"Apologies, gentlemen," Aviva said finally. "The thought of Javi missing makes me paranoid. I didn't mean to burden you with my suspicions."

Levi leaned forward and patted her hand. "Why are you being targeted?"

She clanked the spoon against her cup. "It sounds silly, I'm just on edge because of what happened to Fredrich."

"That's understandable," I said. "I understand Chief Gunderson hasn't been helpful in that investigation."

"I'm . . . I'm being threatened." She released a giant sigh.

"By Gunderson?"

"No. This sounds absurd, but . . . it's Reverend Papadopoulos."

Levi and I exchanged confused glances.

Aviva swallowed and fussed with her robe. "Duncan arrived in town a few weeks before Fredrich disappeared. He seemed friendly enough, but after I was appointed mayor, his behavior toward me became . . . aggressive."

The Duncan I'd met this morning appeared friendly, even a little shy. He'd clearly helped Jenny, and, well, dressing an unconscious me counted in his favor, too. "Aggressive how?"

Aviva tapped her nails against her coffee cup. "Homelessness is on the rise in Austin, and some of that population is being bussed to other places like Bluebonnet Hills. Duncan's solution is to feed, clothe, and house these individuals, but he wants the town to pay for it."

"And the council says no?"

"We're not heartless, but we believe our budget should go to town improvements, such as the revitalization, not pay for problems we didn't create."

I nodded. "Surely Duncan understood the decision, even if he didn't agree with the outcome?"

"That's how it appeared at the council meeting. But then he confronted me, here at the house. I was taking out the trash, and there he was, standing in front of his car, watching from across the street. It frightened me, but I waved, untrained in the etiquette for these situations. He yelled at me, 'I know you've got plenty of money stashed away, I don't know why you can't help.' Then he got in his car, this hideous green hatchback, and drove off."

I stared into my tea. How many hideous green hatchbacks could be in Bluebonnet Hills? Hopefully at least two. "The car circling your drive, when you invited us in? Is that the same car you see around town?" I wrapped my fingers underneath the seat of my chair, bracing for the answer.

"Yes. That was our only confrontation, but I see that car everywhere, at the grocery store, parked on the square. I keep expecting him to jump out at me." She wrapped her arms around herself.

"Who have you told about this?" I asked. "Chief Gunderson? Deputy Perkins, perhaps?"

"Perkins works for Gunderson," she said flatly. "And the only things Tex and I agree on are mutual dislike and distrust. You have firsthand experience with that, Mr. Tanaka."

"But you still have a homelessness problem, and it seems to have some locals on edge," Levi said. "Those optics can't be good for the revitalization efforts."

"Or a mayoral campaign," I added.

My flip comment temporarily stunned Aviva. "Revitalizing Bluebonnet Hills was my husband's dream. I have no interest in running for mayor. For any political office. I'm serving out Fredrich's term to see his dreams to completion ... hoping he'll come home in the meantime."

"I'm sorry. That was insensitive of me."

She sniffed and gave me a small smile. "It's all politics, Mr. Tanaka. I understand that better than anyone. And you are correct: if I ran for mayor, this problem, and the related spike in crime, would be a thorn in my campaign."

"We found mats, afghans, and food cans at the construction site," I said. "And I encountered a few of the ... er, residents."

Aviva considered this. "Javi usually monitors his sites for that very reason. I suppose it makes sense, though. Duncan wants to torpedo the revitalization, so he uses our sites to advance his cause. I suppose there's some irony there." Her head slumped forward, and for a moment, I thought she'd fallen asleep. When she popped up, her eyes were full of fear. "But I told someone about my confrontation with Duncan: Javi."

"When was this?" I asked.

Aviva searched her memory, which was painful to watch as she looked hungover from the day before. "A few weeks ago, I think. Javi told me not to worry. He said Duncan's passion sometimes eclipsed his kind soul."

Levi cocked his head. "That's pretty specific. Did those two know each other well?"

She shrugged. "It's a small town, but now that you mention it, I hadn't realized they knew each other." Aviva's phone dinged, alerting her to a text message. "You gentlemen will have to excuse me. I need to get on with the rest of my day."

Before we'd finished our drinks, Levi and I stood on the other side of Aviva's front door, which swiftly slammed and locked behind us.

Chapter 12

Jenny's hatchback wasn't parked in front of the Cherry Blossom. I suspected Duncan was still joyriding after terrorizing Aviva Ernst.

"What's the rush?" Levi called after me. "Let's debrief, plot our next move."

I turned, now walking backward. "I'm out of moves. Jenny needs the truth about Duncan. Then she needs to offload this café. Perhaps there'll be money left to enroll her in culinary school. That's the best place for her."

Levi flattened his lips. "You need a script rewrite, soften your line delivery."

I stopped and took a cleansing breath. "I'm sorry we didn't find better answers to your museum questions, but fun and games are over. This is a family matter. Jenny is too trusting; never finds the fault in people."

"Those are admirable qualities."

"Not when it causes self-destruction. Jenny excels with these cloudbursts of inspiration, but she eventually gets drenched in rain and big brother has to step in with an umbrella."

"Has she asked you for help?"

"No… but she will." I pulled the door open with more force than intended, eliciting a strangled jingle from the bell above.

Jenny dropped the rag she was using on the counter. The café was empty, so we wouldn't have an audience.

"Where are the flowers?" Her eyes darted from me to Levi.

Oops. I'd forgotten about her text. "I'll go later," I said, losing some of my momentum.

She brushed a strand of hair behind her ear. "I'll take care of it." And then, a beat later said, "I need to talk to you."

Her comment sidetracked me. Talk to me? About what? Jenny pushed through the swinging doors into the kitchen, my cue to follow.

"Well … I need to talk to *you*." So there.

"I need to eat." Levi raised himself into a swivel chair and grabbed a laminated menu. "Too many choices."

"I'll be back," I said.

"Here's my proposal," Levi said. "We each order our first choice, and then go halfsies. Two meals for one."

"Fine."

"You good with onion rings?"

"Perfect. Discs are easier to hurl at you."

"Meh, I'll just stick with fries …"

I stepped into the kitchen and found Jenny in the walk-in storage closet, her arms crossed. The closet was a little dark, the dim fluorescent light struggling to illuminate the rows of cardboard boxes lined against the wall.

"You first," she said. It was difficult to see her facial expressions, but her tone was terse.

"Were you driving your car this morning? Outside the mayor's house?"

"You already texted me that question. Next question."

My fists clenched. "Where is your car now? Did you let Duncan take it?"

"He's making a bank deposit for me and then getting some groceries. Eggs were popular this morning."

"What do you know about this Duncan?"

"*This* Duncan is a friend, who supports my choices and who runs the occasional errand."

"I'm sorry about the flowers. And I support your choices, the good ones.

"I'm not doing this with you." She moved to leave.

"This? What is this?"

She spun around. "*This* passive-aggressive attitude, about my move here, about the café. It's all so . . . sanctimonious. Particularly coming from you."

"What's that supposed to mean?"

"Ma called this morning."

Uh-oh. I rubbed a hand down my pant leg.

Jenny continued. "She was confirming that her pride and joy made it safely to—what did she call it? Oh yeah, made it safely to Armpit, Texas."

How much did she tell Jenny? "And you were worried Ma was giving you the silent treatment. I'm glad I could reconnect you two. You're welcome."

She pinched the bridge of her nose. "You lost your job?"

"I didn't lose it, it's still there." I heard the catch in my voice.

"You're deflecting. Stop it."

"It's some fiery HR hoop. Mandatory therapy before I can work with patients."

"Therapy? For what?" She touched my arm.

I had told no one in the family about the gun incident in the ICU. I wasn't about to start.

"And Vicky dumped you?" Jenny continued the pile on.

Ma sure was chatty this morning. "We're on pause."

"What does that mean?"

I stepped further into the corner, bumping into a shelf of cleaning supplies. "It's what Victoria called it. On pause."

"She dumped you, Sho. She's a selfish, opportunistic princess. You should have *paused* her years ago."

"Now who's being sanctimonious? Let's return to your dumpster fire of life decisions."

Jenny held up her hands in mock surrender. "I'm actually pretty happy with my decisions."

"Did you know Duncan Papadopoulos is an aggressor? He's been terrorizing the mayor."

"Aviva Ernst is hardly a maiden in a tower. Your fat lip proves she can hold her own."

"Duncan's been harassing her for money, and not taking no for an answer."

Jenny burst out laughing. "The reverend is asking the mayor for money. How scandalous!"

"And he's encouraging the homeless to sleep at Levi's construction site."

"Helping the homeless?" Jenny flopped her hand against her forehead. "Stop, stop before I get the vapors."

"The café's seven percent cash discount? That was Duncan's idea, wasn't it?"

Her jaw clenched. "So what?"

I wrapped my bottom lip over my teeth, calculating how much to say. "I think he's stealing from you."

She held my stare, searching my eyes for truth. "What . . . what's your evidence?"

"It's stuffed inside the wall at Levi's museum."

She blinked. "You sound insane right now."

"That's not fair."

"Oh, it's totally fair. You avoid me for three years, ignore my texts, forget our video chats, and then randomly decide to pop into my life and stick your busted-up nose in my business."

"You're just mad because Ma knew about my job situation and Victoria before you."

"I'm frustrated because this is a convenient enough place for you to hide, but I'm not important enough to trust, to confide in. You share nothing, yet dump all over my decisions."

I raised my voice. "Because decisions have consequences. Quitting school—twice—has consequences. Enabling a string of aimless, stoner boyfriends with less personality and purpose than the mops in this closet has consequences. Sinking money into this café has consequences. You mock me for being snobby and fussy and buttoned-up, but I act this way because I take my responsibilities seriously."

"And what has that gotten you?" she asked quietly. "You're unemployed and single. I own a business, forging my path. And, for the record, I'm doing fan-frigging-tastic in Armpit, Texas. Worry about your own life and stay the hell out of mine."

I looked away. "I'll be gone by morning. I'm done."

She wiped a hand across her face. "See you in another three years."

"Tanaka . . ." Levi stood in the doorway.

Jenny's shoulders raised, and she turned away from both of us. "Not now, Levi."

"Chief Gunderson is here."

I swatted the air with my arm. "If he came to apologize for yesterday, this isn't a great time."

"Sorry, little man, no apology today." Gunderson's capped teeth glowed in the dim lighting of the storage closet. "I need to ask you some questions, both of you." He said the last part to Levi.

"Of course. Would you give us a moment?"

Gunderson sucked in his cheeks. "Don't make me ask you again, please. We can chat in the dining area, privately, or we can stand here and discuss why you were spotted in the car of a convicted drug dealer."

"Sho-chan, what's he talking about?"

When I crossed my arms to hug my waist, my hand brushed against Javi's prescription bottle, still hidden in my pocket. I gulped. "That won't be necessary."

Deputy Perkins waited in the dining area, his arms crossed, standing against the wall like an Easter Island statue. Levi and I took spots near the swivel chairs, exchanging confused glances. Gunderson, still in his shorts, strutted past us. He spun a chair and straddled it backwards. Levi stifled a groan of amusement. The chief certainly painted a vivid picture.

Gunderson said, "Assume I already know the answers to my questions. What were you doing at Aviva Ernst's house this morning?"

I released a nervous laugh, much to the annoyance of the chief. He didn't lead off with questions about the construction site, the wall of money, the episode at Javi's house. This was an easy one to answer. "Levi wanted some information on the museum."

"Do they not use phones in Holly-weird, Mr. Blue?"

Levi smiled. "I prefer the personal touch."

"Were you angry, Mr. Blue? About the museum?"

"I don't get angry. I wanted information on my investment."

"So, you dropped by her house, on a Saturday? Sounds like a load of Hollywood entitlement."

I scuffed my shoe against the floor. "Excuse me, chief, I'm confused. Is the mayor claiming we harassed her? She invited us into her home, served us tea and cocoa. No one was angry. In fact, she shared some things with us."

Gunderson said, "Enlighten me, little man. What things did the mayor share?"

Little man was losing his patience. "If you give us more information, perhaps we can answer your questions more specifically."

Perkins approach Gunderson and whispered in his ear. Gunderson listened, nodded, and then waved the deputy back to his post. Gunderson surveyed us before he announced, "Mayor Ernst has disappeared."

I looked at Levi. "Yes . . . Aviva mentioned that. Do you have some leads on Fredrich's disappearance?"

Gunderson punched his fists into his hips. "Let me be clear, guys: Aviva Ernst has disappeared. And I understand you spoke to her last."

Chapter 13

"WHAT MAKES YOU THINK Aviva is missing?" I asked.

Gunderson flattened a hand against his face, studying me. "A neighbor discovered the front door open. It raised some concerns, so she reported it."

"Let me guess. Was the neighbor Barbara Lou Sinclair?"

Gunderson deferred to his deputy, who gave a slight head shake. "That's not really relevant. It appears a scuffle took place in the home. Several kitchen chairs were knocked over, and we found three cups on the table. You've already confirmed you had coffee with Aviva."

"I had hot chocolate," Levi clarified. I hoped he'd skip the peppermint schnapps part.

I held my palms out. "Chief, I'd never met Aviva Ernst until yesterday. I have no reason to want her to disappear. And Levi's been with me all morning; I can vouch for him."

The corner of Levi's mouth curled into a smile.

Gunderson rubbed his temples. "This entire museum silliness aside, neither of you had an obvious motive." He let out a deep sigh, and the creases in his forehead looked cavernous under the café's fluorescent lights. "I'm here seeking information. If I don't find Aviva, and soon, this town will be swarmed with Texas Rangers. If I'm going to protect y'all, I need to know everything."

I stared at Levi until he was forced to return eye contact. He understood what needed to happen next. He nodded, grudgingly, and I said to the chief, "We might know a few things that could help."

And, so, I told Gunderson about Aviva's fear of Duncan Papadopoulos, about the money at the construction site that Duncan likely stole, probably to fund his initiatives to help the homeless. I also mentioned our theory that Javi Zepeda was missing, glossing over all the events that led us to that conclusion. As I talked, Javi's prescription bottle burned a metaphorical hole in my pocket. When I'd finished, Levi only appeared mildly annoyed and Deputy Perkins again whispered something in the chief's ears.

Gunderson waved Perkins away. "You left the money-in-the-wall part out when you spoke to the deputy earlier." It was a statement, not a question.

"I was shaken up from seeing the gho… the homeless." Which was true. Mostly.

He stared at me, a technique he'd probably used to get people to keep talking, perhaps incriminate themselves. He miscalculated. I loved silence and hadn't had any all day.

"Anything else?" Gunderson asked finally.

I shook my head and Levi gave a half-hearted shrug.

"Well, I can clear up some of your story," Gunderson said. "Javi Zepeda isn't missing, he's retired to St. Augustine."

"Florida? But my museum…"

"I don't know why Aviva didn't tell you that, Mr. Blue. Would have saved everyone some time. Anyway, Javi's moved on. His nephew Tito is packing up the last of his things, clearing out the house before it's put on the market."

Tito. I guessed that was the man formerly known as Scarface. I tried to remember all our discoveries from Javi's house. Levi found a postcard he claimed came from Javi. But the image was of the Golden Gate Bridge, so California not Florida.

"Let us handle the investigating." Gunderson's command brought me back to the present.

"Of course," I said.

Levi turned to me, tugging his earlobe. "The neighbor found Aviva's front door open. But she slammed it behind us, and locked it. Remember?"

I searched my memory of our visit. "I do, it was just after she received the text."

"What text?" The chair groaned when Gunderson shifted his weight.

"Aviva texted someone after Duncan circled the drive," I said. "And someone texted her before we left."

Levi continued. "If she locked the door after we left, she had to have unlocked it later."

"Did you notice a peephole?" I asked him, my voice rising. "Surely she wouldn't open the door for Duncan Papadopoulos. Perhaps it wasn't him."

Levi grabbed my shoulders. "Maybe it wasn't anyone. Maybe the stress got to Aviva, and she just walked out on her own."

I raised slightly on my tiptoes, matching his excitement. "But that wouldn't explain the evidence of the kitchen scuffle. Aviva let someone in—"

"Whoa, whoa, whoa." Gunderson waved his arms in the air. "This is *exactly* what I'm talking about. Leave the investigating to us. I don't need you playing *Murder, He Tap Danced* in my town. Lie low, read a book, get a hobby. Me? I knit."

Did I hear that correctly?

"You knit?" Levi asked.

"Knit, crochet, even bake when the mood strikes." As Gunderson listed his hobbies off on his fat fingers, I got a mental image of him making doilies with a cup of hot chocolate and a cat named Mr. Skimbleshanks. "I was raised by a single mama and five older sisters. I'm not afraid to embrace my feminine side." He directed his toothy grin at me. "You understand that, little man. You're a male nurse." He made a finger gun gesture. No *pow-pow* sound effect this time.

I had adaptive immunity to male nurse jokes. Bring it.

Gunderson swung his legs out and stood up from the chair. The flex fabric of his shorts thankfully allowed for an incredible range of motion. "Mr. Blue, you're staying at the Bluebonnet Inn? And you, Tanaka, staying here with your little sister?"

I looked toward the kitchen. Jenny had yet to make an appearance. "Uh, I'll be staying at the inn too."

Gunderson strutted to the exit. Perkins followed several feet behind.

Multiple questions bubbled in my head, but one had risen to the surface. "Chief, how did you know we went to Aviva's house this morning?"

Gunderson turned and squinted. "You told me."

I shook my head. "You knew before we told you. That's how you ended up here."

He flashed a brilliant smile before delivering his exit line.

"For now, I believe you and Mr. Blue had nothing to do with the disappearance of Aviva Ernst. Let's call a truce and move on."

I studied Deputy Perkins, whose expressionless face conveyed nothing. I suspected he'd tailed us after we left the construction site. Which meant he'd followed us to Javi's house. But our breaking-and-entering episode never came up. Was Perkins saving that for leverage? I glanced again at the kitchen before crossing toward the staircase that led to the upstairs bedrooms.

"Where are you going?" Levi asked.

The bottom stair creaked. "To pack, to book a flight home."

"I overheard your argument with Jenny, kind of hard not to. You okay?"

The argument had felt cathartic. Now I wanted to erase its existence, carry on as if it'd never happened. "Yeah. It was a long time coming."

"So, you're leaving her here? With Aviva missing, with all that we learned today?"

"I shared my suspicions about Duncan, that he's using this cash discount to steal money. My conscience is clear."

"Gunderson said not to leave town."

I laughed. "Since when do you follow rules?"

"I don't, but being ethical seems important to you."

"I'll stop by the police station later and ask permission to leave." My face throbbed and fatigue had kicked in. I'd need a nap first.

"Ask Perkins. He seems to be the chief-of-police-whisperer."

I started to take the next step, but stopped. "You're wrong about one thing, Levi. I'm not that ethical." I handed him the prescription bottle from my pocket.

Levi's lips pinched as he studied the label. "Where did you get this?"

"I stole it… from Javi's house. It's empty, but had it been full, I would have taken every pill."

"You take these?"

"I have anxiety."

"About what?"

"Life." I shifted my feet. "And since I'm in a confessional mood, when you saw me at the festival, in Scarface's car? I wasn't confronting him, I was trying to buy some of those." I gestured to the bottle, which Levi handed back.

"You don't need these, you need a new mindset."

"Noted, Dr. Blue. Is that diagnosis based on your almost forty-five minutes of medical training?"

"Positive thinking brings positive results. It's simple math."

I gripped the stair rail. "Simple math aside, I don't think positivity would help me here. I mean, you're irritatingly upbeat, and where has that gotten you? You spent three quarters of a million and mortgaged your family home on a museum that may never be built."

"But I met my new best bud. He's kind of squawky and irritatingly ethical, but that's part of the charm."

I focused on the dark hallway above the staircase. "All part of our comedy dynamic, right? But you wouldn't want to be my friend if you knew me better, knew what I'd done."

"How many pills did you take today?"

"None. I took one at the airport on Thursday and then lost my last one at the festival, when I tripped over that dog."

"How often did you want one today?"

"You mean besides this incident?" I shook the pill bottle. "Not as much as I normally would, I concede. But I've also been too busy getting sucker punched, flung against a tree, accosted by colorful ghosts, and maintaining my balance on a space-age contraption."

"Precisely, too busy having madcap adventures. More madcap

with hijinks and shenanigans, as needed." He shook his pointer finger at me. "That's my medical opinion."

"I don't have the stamina for madcap. I guess that makes me a lousy sidekick. Clearly, I'm no Nanny Sherbets."

"At least you made it out with all your limbs." Levi stubbed the toe of his boot into the floor. "So, that's it then?"

"That's it. There's enough chaos demanding my attention in Seattle. Mostly, I feel foolish, thinking I could escape here, that my responsibilities would disappear. These are the consequences for having no plan." I started back up the stairs. "Good luck, Levi. This unforgettable day will give me night terrors for the rest of my life."

I BARRICADED MYSELF against the bedroom door. I released the breath I'd held up the stairs, exhaling slowly, enjoying the first moments to myself since morning. The ceiling fan hummed above me; my sweet, sweet, ambient siren.

I scanned the room, laughing out loud when I realized there was nothing to pack. However, hanging over the wardrobe was a plastic dry cleaner bag. Hello, pale and tragic duds. Goodbye, busted-up rodeo clown.

After I'd changed, I fired up the Wild West Airlines app on my phone and found a flight leaving Austin for Seattle at 6:30 P.M. There'd be no time for a power nap, but I could still make it to the police station and beg for permission to go home. The app provided no additional updates on my lost bag. Even if it arrived in Texas, I wouldn't be around to receive it.

At random, I pulled open one of the fifteen doors on the *kusuri tansu* and deposited Javi's prescription bottle. Jenny's next guest might find it and wonder why it was there.

I pushed the door shut and wondered: if Javi had left town,

why was his medicine cabinet filled with empty bottles? I'd treated several patients who carried their medication in a single bottle for convenience. Unfortunately, this often led to misidentification, which had many health complications. Javi might have merged everything, but if I was moving to Florida, I'd want an inventory of all my medication.

I found myself back in the upstairs hallway. I noticed the light shining under Jenny's door, soft music playing. I hesitated, but then stepped toward the door, the hardwood floors creaking as I went. I raised my fist to knock. Then stopped. Was there anything left to say? Thanks for the hospitality, I still think you made a terrible mistake moving here? I lowered my hand and stepped away.

I walked back down the hall, doing an initial skim of the day's emails on my phone. I found the earlier text from Jenny, asking me to pick up the centerpieces for the café. I clicked on the hyperlink of the address and realized the florist was less than a ten-minute walk. Well, it was the least I could do.

When I exited the café, there was Levi Blue. He sat on a bench, his hands pressed under his chin.

"What took you so long?"

Chapter 14

I DIRECTED LEVI'S ATTENTION to the sign for the Red Poppy. "I'm here for flowers, that's it."

"I understand what you're saying." He nodded, but his tone sounded cryptic.

"Hmm. I'm serious. No investigating, no madcap chicanery or whatever."

"I understand the words coming out of your mouth."

Perhaps he was a better actor than I'd imagined. I opened the painted red door, saw the woman behind the counter, and spun around. It was the scowling customer I'd encountered the first night at the café.

I pointed and said to Levi, "That lady? She does not like me."

Levi raised his chin. "That can't be an unfamiliar experience."

I squared my shoulders and turned. The flower shop was filled with a garden freshness that should have been bottled up and sold; fresh-cut greens mixed with the dewdrop blooms of roses, freesias, lilacs, and peonies. The scowling customer looked from her salad and magazine. Her mouth widened into a smile. She'd let her hair down, and the color now appeared more honey than dirty dishwater. Her flowered tunic also softened her appearance.

"Well, howdy there, hun. You here for those centerpieces?"

Howdy? Hun? What sick, twisted game was this lady playing?

She snapped the lid on her salad. "Just give me a sec to run on back to—" Her cornflower blue eyes drifted past me and widened. "Oh, oh, oh, my stars! It's you!" She squealed and then said to me, "It's him!"

Levi bowed his head and gave a finger twirl. "Yes, yes, 'tis I."

"I can't believe you're really here." She asked me, "Do you believe he's really here?"

Oh, I believed it.

The woman practically bolted from the counter. Levi extended his hand in greeting, but she wrapped her arms around him. When she backed away, she reached up and cupped his face, tears in her eyes. "You look so much like your daddy."

Levi's posture straightened with surprise. "You… you knew my dad?"

"Everyone knew Little Beau Blue. That's what we called Beau, like *Little Boy Blue*."

"Tanaka, my dad had a nickname!" His lower body jiggled, his feet dancing.

I smiled. It was unexpected and tender, and I felt like an intruder at this private moment.

"I was real sorry to read what happened to him," she said. "I didn't know your momma, but she must be a real special lady to end up with a man like Beau." She tweaked his nose. "And you are one special young man. I saw the resemblance on the TV, but in person, now that you're all grown up, it's clear you are Beau Blue's son."

"Th-thank you." Levi had a catch in his voice. "How did you know my dad?"

"We grew up together. Oh, my manners. I'm Abilene Schubert." She grabbed Levi's hand and squeezed it.

I asked, "Your dad grew up in Bluebonnet Hills?"

"He moved away right before high school when he went to Hollywood. This place was special to him." Levi pinched his mouth to board up his emotion.

"He was an actor, too?" Of course, Levi's attachment to Bluebonnet Hills extended beyond some fan museum or shooting location. He had roots here.

Abilene held out her other hand to me. "I've been wanting to meet you too, Sho, but our paths never crossed."

I tilted my head but gave her my hand to squeeze. Perhaps she was just having a bad day when I first saw her at the café.

Abilene returned to the counter, kicking a bucket as she rounded a corner. "Ignore this mess." She glared at the ceiling and adjusted the bucket. "All this rain we've been having is causing a leak. Again."

I looked up and watched a water droplet plunk into the bucket. I hadn't noticed when we walked in, but my nostrils now twitched from the stench of mildew masked by the fresh florals.

"Here you are." Abilene placed a box on the counter. "There's another box, but give me a second. Gotta catch my breath."

"Here, let me." Levi dashed to grab the second box.

"What a dear," she said. "Now, I packed some newspaper around the vases, but Jenny should unpack everything as soon as she gets them."

"I'll tell her." I peered into the box. The vases overflowed with the colors of a sun-drenched field. The flowers were variegated and contrasted in height and stride, some taller than others, but all lush, healthy, and blooming.

Abilene pulled out a calculator with jumbo-sized buttons. "Lemme just add up the bill."

I pulled the debit card from my wallet and set it on the counter.

Her eyes shot up. "Oh, you're paying with a card? No problem, dear, but I won't be able to give you the discount."

It took several seconds to process what she'd said. "Discount? Do you offer a seven percent cash discount?"

"Lucky number seven."

I nervously pushed the debit card across the counter, watching the water drop into the bucket. "Abilene. Do the other shops offer the same discount?"

"Uh-huh. Hoyt uses it at the gift shop, and I think the car wash is cash-only too."

Levi placed the second box of centerpieces next to the first. "All Reverend Papadopoulos's idea?"

Abilene's face brightened at the mention of the reverend's name. "Why, yes. He offered to teach me the computer, but he made it all sound too complicated. Cash is easier, and it doesn't get those viruses or need updates."

"Does the reverend help with your ledgers, too?" I asked.

She clasped her hands together. "He's a doll, and paper is much easier for me to keep track of." She spun the calculator to show me the total amount.

I watched another droplet plop into the bucket. "Do you own this space?"

"Most of us rent. Jenny lucked out because Javi owned and operated the café." She hefted a clunky credit card machine to the counter. It was one of those manual flatbed contraptions that was apparently still in circulation.

"And Javi is your property manager?"

She fitted my card and a slip of paper into the machine. "He's the only game in town." The machine made a zip-zap sound when Abilene swept the handle back and forth. "And he still hasn't fixed this roof." She inspected the imprint on the paper and gave herself a congratulatory nod before handing me my copy.

"How long have you had this leak?"

She glared again at the ceiling. "It's a pretty regular thing, but we've had a lot of rain this month. Javi's pretty handy, but he's always jumping on new business opportunities, so he can be slow to fix things."

"You have other repairs?" I asked. "Besides the leak?"

The tip of Abilene's tongue stuck out as she compiled a mental list. "Seems like there are always electrical issues, and the pipes are old. Comes with the bones of the building. But the grant money should help me get everything sorted."

Levi adjusted the boxes on the counter, shooting me a look. "Oh, you got some grant money? How nice."

"Javi helped me get it. It's money from the government just for women business owners. I can use it for repairs and upkeep, those sorts of things."

"How much of that money have you spent?"

"None yet. Javi said he'd manage it. He's doing the repairs himself, so I can stretch the money for other things." She rolled her eyes. "My big sister says I'm a fool. She says Javi takes advantage of me. Sisters can be such a pain."

I could relate. "When did you see Javi last?"

Abilene tapped a finger on her chin. "Before the festival. I was swamped with orders the two weeks before." She bent down and pulled out a flip phone, also with jumbo buttons. "Come to think of it, I texted him to fix this leak."

Levi stretched his neck to read Abilene's phone. "Did he respond?"

She squinted at the screen. "He replied, 'Can't. Cedar fever.'"

Another nonsensical message from Javi. "Not very helpful."

"He's had it before." She stage-whispered to Levi, "Serves him right for sneaking into Austin. That's where he gets it, you know?"

I shook my head. "Sorry, this… cedar fever? That's a thing?"

Levi nodded. "It's pollen allergies from the cedar trees. Miserable."

"Comes from Austin." Abilene sniffed.

"Uh, okay. What are the symptoms of cedar fever?"

"Depends on the person, but Javi had it real bad. Dry hack, runny nose, body aches, even lost some weight. But, like I said, he's always running around…" She drifted off, her eyes sparkled with mischief. "Are y'all on a case?"

"Absolutely!"

"No. We are absolutely not on a case," I said.

"Oooh, goody." Abilene grabbed Levi's arm. "What's the case? Do you need a sidekick? I can be your Texas nanny sidekick." She held her hands in the air. "I could be Nanny Lonestar."

"Perfect. A detective can never have too many sidekicks," Levi said. "Unless they get better jokes or wardrobe."

"So, the text?" I asked, redirecting the conversation. "That was your last communication with Javi?"

"Besides the postcard." She rifled through a stack of papers on a workstation. "Here it is."

I read it. "'Gone Fishing. X.'"

"That's the same message I found on the postcard from…" Levi cut himself off before confessing to our earlier break-in.

"'X' is for Xavier," Abilene said, unaware of Levi's near-snafu. "But I didn't call him that."

The postcard depicted a white sandy beach and swaying palm trees. It looked familiar. Where had I seen the image before? I flipped the card over, and there was Levi grimacing back at me. Rather, it was Billy the Kid, the Wild West Air goat that Levi voiced. I flashed the postcard to Levi, whose crooked grin mirrored Billy's.

"I've got boxes of those." He took the card from me to admire. "They make great stocking stuffers."

"Who else sells these besides the airline?"

"Everyone, rest stops, gas stations. Billy is a travel icon."

"Where did Gunderson say Javi had retired?"

"Florida. St. Augustine, maybe."

"Did you say Javi retired?" Abilene's hands shot out and gripped the counter. The news had surprised her. "When was this?"

I exchanged glances with Levi. "I don't know exactly. Chief Gunderson seemed to imply it was a recent move; Javi's house isn't even on the market yet. But Javi never mentioned this to you? His other renters?"

Abilene shook her head slowly, still processing the news. "Noooo… Javi's never even mentioned the word *retirement*. That sounds too much like *quitting*, and I don't see him sitting still for long. And why Florida? He's lived in Bluebonnet Hills almost his entire life."

"Can I see that card again?" I asked Levi. The image of the white beach certainly had a better chance of being in Florida than the Golden Gate Bridge card from Javi's house. I flipped the card over and leaned in. "Levi, look here." I pointed to the stamp from the post office, its black ink running over the original postage stamp. "Its location is stamped Austin, Texas. This card didn't leave the state."

Abilene tsk-ed at the mention of Austin.

"Did Javi have other family in the area?" I asked Abilene. "Someone who might inherit his real estate businesses?"

She stared at the wall in front of her, obviously panicked over how her business would survive without Javi's help. "He doesn't have much close family. I remember mention of a nephew, but I don't think it was anything good."

That matched what I already knew about Tito, aka Scarface.

Abilene continued. "Javi has a son he occasionally mentions, but I don't think they see each other much. Calista left Texas when she divorced Javi. She moved to the Midwest, but that was thirty years ago. Maybe the son lives in Florida now."

I considered all this out loud. "Javi retires, seemingly abruptly, and moves to a place that doesn't hold any obvious ties. Then residents receive cards from him, or someone claiming to be him, that are all postmarked from within the state."

"It all sounds pretty strange. What are you thinking?" Levi asked.

"I'm not convinced Javi Zepeda retired to Florida. In fact, I'm wondering if he might be dead."

Chapter 15

THE BACK DOOR of the Red Poppy burst open.

"Barbara Lou, I'm glad you're safe. That was a risky move on your part." The voice was female, but her face was hidden behind the box she carried, heaped with spray bottles and rags, the handle of a black bucket dangling from her arm.

When she turned to set the box down, I noticed a Bluetooth device in her ear. She continued the phone conversation. "I'll see what I can dig up, and thanks for the lead." She listened to the caller, fidgeting with the spray bottles. "No, no, I won't quote you. You be safe now." She disconnected from the call and spun toward Abilene.

"Sister, here's the cleaning supplies you wanted. I'm leaving for the office. Aviva Ernst is missing."

Abilene's hands flew to her face. "Oh, my. That's just awful."

The woman furrowed her brow and touched Abilene's cheek. "You're pale… and clammy. What's wrong?"

Abilene patted her sister's hand. "I've had a little shock of my own. Javi Zepeda retired to Florida." She gestured to me. "And Sho here thinks he might be dead."

"Dead?" The woman scowled at us, confirming she was the unpleasant customer from the café. And Abilene's identical twin sister.

"Twins," Levi said, making the same connection. "*Older* sister." He teased Abilene.

"You've been telling that same tired tale for fifty-eight years," the woman said to her twin. "Older. By four minutes."

Abilene's cheeks bloomed with amusement. "Boys, this is Odessa, editor of the *Bluebonnet Bee*. And my grumpy, *older* sister."

"I'm not grumpy, I'm direct."

Levi patted my shoulder. "You should steal that line."

"What paper do you work for?" Odessa set down the bucket she was carrying. "What's the angle of this investigation?"

I wrapped my arms around a box of centerpieces. "I'm here for flowers. No one is investigating anything."

"We had coffee with the mayor this morning. Right before she disappeared," Levi added, ever so helpful.

Odessa fished a small spiral notebook from her coat pocket and flipped it open. "Can I ask you a few questions?"

Levi stepped forward and cleared this throat. "I was born in the Hollywood Hills with stars in my eyes and a surprising amount of ambidexterity…."

Abilene clapped in anticipation of Levi's origin story.

"That's not what she wants to ask." I released my hold on

the box. I asked Odessa, "You've covered the news here for some time?"

She gave a curt nod. "I've edited the *Bee* for nine years. Before that, I taught high school English. I know everyone in this town and their grammatical deficiencies." While her sister's voice was light and ethereal, Odessa's growl transmitted she was a two-pack-a-day smoker.

"Would you agree this town has some… uh, questionable ethics with its finances?"

Odessa's lips puckered. "I have some suspicions." She flipped the cover back over her notebook. "I'll share some of them, off the record, but first tell me your take on Aviva's disappearance."

I considered which events to highlight. "Aviva was fearful of Duncan Papadopoulos. He threatened her and followed her around town. Something to do with using town funds to help the homeless. Perhaps Duncan was involved with the mayor's disappearance."

"I don't believe it," Abilene said. "The reverend is a prince."

"We both sit on the council," Odessa said, including her sister. "I recall the meeting about the homeless, but I wouldn't characterize Duncan as angry. Passionate, perhaps, but he's always seemed a little vanilla to me."

That was my impression of Duncan, too. It still didn't explain why the mild-mannered reverend was at the mayor's house this morning. Officially, I didn't see the hatchback's driver, so perhaps I incorrectly assumed it was him. "Aviva said he threatened her after the meeting."

Odessa considered this. "Possible, I suppose. But, you saw Aviva's courthouse confrontation at the festival. She has a dramatic quality."

"She seemed frightened," Levi said.

I said, "Duncan is helping my sister with her café's finances. I'm leery of some of his business advice, such as this seven percent cash discount. Levi and I found some evidence at the construction site that the reverend might be funding his philanthropic activities with stolen cash."

Odessa glared at her sister. "That discount baloney never made sense to me."

Abilene shrugged. "You suspect everybody of everything."

"That means I'm never wrong." She looked at me. "Any other thoughts on Aviva?"

I gave a slight shrug. "Levi suggested Aviva left on her own, that the stress of her husband's disappearance consumed her. I was surprised at how quickly Gunderson responded to the scene." I pointed to the Bluetooth device still perched around Odessa's ear. "But it sounds like Barbara Lou Sinclair is the neighborhood phone tree."

Odessa asked. "What's your impression of Gunderson?"

"He seems very fond of himself," I said. "I suppose that makes him an effective politician."

"Sometimes he comes to our knitting circle," Abilene said. "I like to just sit and watch him work. He so… sinewy." Her lashes fluttered.

Odessa curled her lip. "Aviva's worried he'll run for mayor again. He could win."

"Run again?" Levi asked. "Did he run against Fredrich Ernst?"

"He tried, but Fredrich marched into that race with his DC machine and donor money. It became a David and Goliath scenario, with Tex getting toppled."

"Election wasn't even close," Abilene said.

"I bet that bruised Gunderson's ego." And then I added, "But Aviva isn't running for mayor. That's what she told us, anyway."

Odessa leveled her gaze at me. "Hmm. Well-placed sources in her administration tell me otherwise."

"Tex's got my vote," Abilene said, returning from her thoughts of sinewy knitting. "Unless you run for mayor, Levi. You'll always be my number one."

"Ha ha, me as mayor. Can you imagine?"

"What was Gunderson's relationship with Fredrich Ernst?" I asked "There must be some mutual respect there; Ernst appointed his political rival chief of police."

"There wasn't much rivalry, at least not for Fredrich," Odessa said. "I think he saw Tex less a threat than a decent cop who could maintain order here. Any friction between those two stemmed from Tex's job performance."

Abilene sighed. "Grab your tinfoil, boys, and hunker down for some conspiracy theories."

Odessa tugged at her bottom lip and responded in a low voice. "Sister doesn't believe me, but there's truth to the fraud Aviva alleged at the festival. I think Tex was fudging the crime statistics."

"To make the town look safer?"

"To make it look worse." Odessa nudged her sister. "Tell them about the bouquet incident."

Levi propped his elbows on the counter to cradle his head.

Abilene sighed. "It's all a silly misunderstanding. Barbara Lou Sinclair hired me to create bouquets for her niece's wedding. It was short notice, something fell through with the original florist." She sniffed, so I assumed the florist was from Austin. "Well, I did what I could, and they came out just beautiful."

I nodded along with Abilene, wondering what flower bouquets had to do with crime statistics.

She continued. "Barbara Lou didn't like that I used pink evening primrose. She hates pink. Well, it wasn't her wedding, but I thought the broad petals looked so pretty woven into the bouquets, and—"

"Move it along, Sister."

"Barbara Lou said the bouquets looked cheap, something a… a… oh, what word did she use?"

"Trollop."

"Thank you, Sister. Something a trollop would have. And I said to Barbara Lou, well, it *is* your niece's third wedding."

Impressive burn. "I bet that made her eyes bug right out of her skull," I said.

Both Schubert sisters released an involuntary laugh.

"That's when it happened," Abilene said when she'd recovered. "She kind of… chucked a bouquet at me."

"Barbara Lou Sinclair sounds delightful," I said. "How does this relate to the crime stats?"

"We print the police blotter in the paper." Odessa took control of the conversation. "There was no simple assault reported, but there was an aggravated assault."

The explanation was still circling the runway. My expression must have communicated that.

Odessa continued. "Let's say I threw a shoe at Sho, but it bounced off. That's reported as simple assault."

Levi laughed. "'Threw a shoe at Sho.' That's a tongue twister. Try saying that three times fast."

And then he and Abilene tried.

"But if that shoe damaged your eye, or you needed stitches, that's aggravated assault," said Odessa.

I mashed my eyebrows together. "So, Abilene was a victim of assault with a deadly wedding bouquet?"

"Exactly."

"And this misreporting… it became a pattern? Are you sure it wasn't some mix-up, a clerical error?"

"That's the excuse Gunderson gave when I asked. But Bluebonnet Hills has less than 2,000 people. At least one person knows everything that happens here. It was too deliberate to be a clerical error." Odessa turned to the workstation and thumbed through a stack of newspapers her sister repurposed as packing supplies.

"Why would a police chief inflate his town's crime statistics?" Levi asked. "That only makes him look incompetent."

"Not if they stop that crime wave." Odessa threw down a newspaper. The headline to the lead story read, "BBH Police receive $250K grant for community policing development."

"Money, money, money," Levi sang, reading over my shoulder.

"This is federal money." Odessa's lip curled. "Like the money you got for the flower shop but have never seen, Sister."

"And it was awarded to create programs to deter crime?" I asked.

Odessa held her hands out and shrugged. "But if there was no crime to begin with—"

"—it would be easier to show results and misappropriate those funds." I shook my head in disbelief. Was Gunderson this clever? Or was Perkins the one whispering these ideas in his ear? "Did you confront Gunderson with your hunch?"

"I went to Fredrich Ernst. He expressed concern, as I assumed he would. The Ernst family were early settlers of Bluebonnet Hills, going back to the 1840s. He received the information with an open mind and vowed to investigate it."

"I'm guessing he didn't?"

"I suspect he did. He disappeared a few weeks later, and Gunderson got his revenge. He stopped letting the paper print the police blotter."

I glanced at Levi. "Uh, how is that revenge?"

"We're partial to our police blotters here," Abilene said. "They tell us what's going on in town and often give a chuckle or two. That's why most of us read the paper. No offense, Sister."

"Subscriptions dropped twenty percent," Odessa said. "That was only the first week."

"You think Gunderson knew you were onto his scheme, so he tried to sink the paper?"

Odessa adjusted her bun. "His official comment was that the blotter reflected poorly on the department, making his officers look inept by responding to frivolous calls about missing cats."

Could Gunderson be the one storing money at the construction site? If so, why? The small, random denominations of cash we found still puzzled me. Those amounts would more logically come from a business, like a café or a flower shop, not the federal government.

"Sister, I just remembered," Abilene said. "Tex and Fredrich had a rivalry of sorts. In high school."

Odessa hid her expression with her hand. "There's almost fifteen years in age between them, Sister. They were never in high school at the same time."

"They were both swimmers. Tex was swim team captain, and he barely missed beating that state record—"

"That Fredrich Ernst had set years before, I remember now." Odessa gave me a wry smile. "I guess they were rivals. Even back in high school, Tex couldn't beat Ernst."

"Gunderson is a swimmer." I rubbed my chin. "At least that's one mystery solved."

Everyone looked at me quizzically.

"Gunderson's lack of body hair, the shaved arms and legs. Swimmers shave their hair to move faster in the water." I looked at Levi, whose rocker lips plumped with confusion. "What? You never did an episode where you posed as an uncoordinated synchronized swimmer sent to stop a corrupt merman from sabotaging the water ballet *Slippery When Wet*?"

"No, but we needed that level of brilliance in the writers' room."

"What's your theory on Xavier Zepeda?" Odessa asked.

"I taught him in sophomore English class. He loved to misplace his modifiers, but he had a good heart."

"It's all circumstantial. In Javi's house—never mind how we got there—Levi and I found a device that measures your blood oxygen levels. It's a useful tool for patients with lung disease."

"There was a standing fan also, facing the recliner." Levi looked at me. "Is that another clue?"

I nodded. "Some research has found fan use can reduce the feeling of breathlessness."

"So Javi had a lung condition?"

I nodded. "Based on his long-term career in construction, I'd guess he had mesothelioma."

"Cancer?" Odessa asked.

"Oh, that poor, poor man," Abilene added.

"The symptoms that Abilene described, for the cedar fever—those are consistent with mesothelioma. Patients often think it's a cold or allergies, so they wait too long to see a doctor."

"Maybe Javi's not dead," Levi suggested. "Maybe he disappeared to Austin to get treatment."

I considered this, but it didn't seem likely. "Gunderson said his nephew was cleaning out Javi's house, getting it ready to sell. Mesothelioma is often diagnosed in its later stage. It can be impossible to remove the cancer, even with surgery."

"Perhaps he disappeared to die alone, not to burden anyone," Odessa said.

"Adds a darker meaning to his message on the postcards, 'Gone Fishing,'" Levi added.

"Or… perhaps someone harmed him." Odessa again thumbed through the stack of paper and threw a second one on the table. "This is from a former student who writes for a newspaper in Del Rio." Odessa tapped her finger on a mugshot. "Do you recognize this guy?"

"Scarface, I mean, Tito." I studied the photo. "This is Javi's nephew."

"Tito Ramirez. He also has a record of aggravated assault and robbery, and he's been linked to human trafficking and smuggling migrants across the border."

"Do you think that's happening in Bluebonnet Hills?" I looked at Levi. "Those ghosts… er, figures I encountered at the construction site. I thought they were homeless, but could they be migrants?"

He shrugged. "Better chance of that than the supernatural."

"Have we been thinking about this all wrong?" I asked. "If Tito is smuggling migrants across the border, he'd need somewhere to keep them hidden. Aviva said Javi monitored his sites specifically to keep them safe, keep people from squatting there. But perhaps Javi knew what his nephew was doing. Perhaps he was even helping." I looked at the Schubert sisters. "Does that behavior match your impressions of Javi?"

Odessa opened her mouth to answer, but Abilene spoke first. "Absolutely not, no."

"Now, Sister, you don't—"

"I do, I do know. Javi came to this country legally. That was a point of pride for him. But he has a heart. He understands the terror in the world, the lengths people will go to escape that terror. He also knows that people exploit that terror. But he hates, just hates, the conditions those migrants bear when crossing the border. Barbaric, vile, he's told me. No, if Javi knew what his nephew was doing, he'd have spoken up."

"Maybe he did," Levi said.

Odessa nodded. "With his uncle gone, and mayors coming and going, Tito Ramirez could run this town. And make a healthy profit."

Chapter 16

THE CLOSED SIGN hung on the window of the Cherry Blossom. I twisted the door handle and banged on the glass. "Come on, Jenny, open the door."

Levi set a box of centerpieces on the bench. "Text her again. Maybe she'll open up for flowers."

I stared at my phone, willing those typing bubbles to appear under my message. "Her car's still missing. I'm worried."

Levi slumped on the bench, stretching out his long legs. "Duncan could still be driving around, terrorizing the town. Or Jenny has the car and went to clear her head."

"Where? Where would she go?" My voice raised an octave.

Levi flinched. "I… uh, maybe the river? There are some scenic spots close by, to sit and think." He wiped his brow, his breathing heavy from hefting a box from the flower shop.

I was breathing hard too. I shrugged off my blazer and hung it on the back of a rocking chair. The combination of the humidity and my frustrations was giving me a case of the underarm sweats.

"Something triggered you at the flower shop, got you anxious. What is it?"

I perched on the edge of the rocking chair. "The first night I was here, Jenny told me how the Ernsts 'discovered' her. Coincidentally, they were in New Jersey for her culinary school theme night."

"Fredrich represented a district in Jersey," Levi said.

"Yeah. But this human trafficking ring that Odessa mentioned? What if the Ernsts were scouting prospects? Is that why they recruited Jenny?"

Levi rubbed his chin and considered this. "A beautiful young woman in her twenties gets a fantastic offer for a café in a small town—"

"—in a state she's never visited. To isolate her, basically. Jenny's chatty, so she might have mentioned her strained relationship with Ma, and, well… perhaps with me. It could create the false impression that she doesn't have much of a family."

"Making it easier for her to disappear," Levi said. "I see where your mind is going."

"You're the eternal optimist here, tell me I'm wrong. Tell me I'm being paranoid and analytical. Tell me to join the tinfoil hat club with Odessa. Please."

"You definitely think too much. But you're not considering that Jenny has a survivalist's instinct; she's no dummy. Plus, your theory assumes Fredrich and Aviva were co-conspirators. Why? What's their motive?"

"They hold all the power. We've uncovered several pots of

money, but each is controlled by a different source. Javi controls the commercial real estate and manages these small business grants."

"And Gunderson got the police safety grant. How much was that, a quarter million?"

"Sounds right. Tito Ramirez has a history of human smuggling, namely migrants from Mexico. There's another money pot. What are we missing?"

"The infamous wall of money that might belong to the good godly Reverend Papadopoulos."

I lurched forward in the rocking chair, almost catapulting myself off. "Right, the mastermind behind the seven percent cash discount. That's four pots, all controlled by different people, bringing me back to the Ernsts. The mayor holds all the power."

"The mayor appoints the chief of police, the mayor reviews all the bids for construction projects, the mayor can move and reallocate parts of the budget."

"And both these mayors have disappeared."

Levi scrunched his face. "So, their plan all along was to defraud the town? Then they staggered their disappearances to misdirect, make it seem like foul play."

"Exactly."

"But where does Javi fit? We believe he's disappeared too, possibly even dead. Has your theory evolved there?"

My eyes drifted across the town square. The headlights of a police cruiser poked out from the low-hanging branches of a live oak. "Don't turn around, but we're being watched."

Levi's face twitched to control the impulse to turn. "Chief Gunderson?"

"Deputy Perkins, I bet." The Segways were still where we parked them. "Those spots, near the river? Can we get there on the Segways and shake Perkins?"

"I thought you had a flight to catch."

"Just a quick pit stop."

LEVI GUIDED US through a path that led to a spot near the river that snaked behind the Ernst McMansion. We parked the Segways under some trees to protect them from the spitting rain. I rested my hands on the rock wall that separated us from the Guadalupe. It was wide and lazy, and even in high tide its green waters looked tame compared to the residents of Bluebonnet Hills.

"Remind me what Javi texted you. The message about the *terrible mustache*." I closed my eyes and tilted my face to the sky. The occasional plop of rain offered some relief from the sticky heat.

Levi sat at an aluminum picnic table under a pavilion. He had stretched out his long legs and propped his boots on the opposite bench. He read the message: "'I regret my terrible mustache. Need your platinum to give me courage.'"

"I'm convinced Javi meant *mistake* instead of *mustache*. Let's decipher *platinum* then… I need your platinum to give me courage." I tugged at my blazer buttons. "Perhaps he meant *platform*."

"'I need your platform to give me courage?' What does that mean?"

I opened my eyes and turned around. "Your platform… your celebrity status. You're connected to this town, through your dad, through your show. Dare I say it, you have credibility here."

Levi's lips curved. "How would my celebrity and connections give Javi courage?"

"He wanted to confess something. That's what he meant about his mistake. And he wanted assurances his big reveal would earn him some media attention."

"Why not go straight to Odessa, then?"

I held my hands out and shrugged. "He wanted more than

local media. Perhaps the more people who knew his secret, the less likely he'd be killed over it."

"Not only is Javi dead, someone murdered him?"

"Only considering all scenarios. If the Ernsts were defrauding the town, they'd want the help of a childhood friend with real estate connections. That could also explain why Fredrich Ernst ditched a well-connected job in DC for here. Sleepy Texas towns provide excellent cover for your crimes."

"So, they used Javi's real estate connections to help defraud the town, and then disposed of him when they got what they wanted? I guess that fits. That theory also fits for Tito Ramirez. He used his uncle's connections to advance his human smuggling scheme—"

"—and then disposed of him." I considered Javi's empty pill bottle I'd left in a drawer of the *kusuri tansu*. Tito had probably raided his uncle's pill supply to resell to the town youth. Or losers like me. My stomach churned at how close I came to buying a sick man's pills.

Levi said, "You know, the simpler solution is someone wanted to eliminate the Ernsts and Javi. Odessa said it—with them all gone, Tito Ramirez could cash in."

The air smelled of damp stone and wet wood, and the river itself rolled with a quiet rumble. I clutched my phone through my pocket, hoping for a reply from Jenny. It felt silly to pray she was only angry and ignoring me. The alternatives seemed worse. "I don't know, Levi. Tito couldn't orchestrate much without Gunderson getting wind of it. The chief's biceps may be bigger than his brain, but Tito's on his radar."

"Unless Gunderson is helping him. Or maybe Tito and Deputy Perkins are working together. The deputy didn't exactly raid the construction site when you told him what we found. He tailed us instead."

True, Perkins seemed to have a silent authority in Bluebonnet

Hills. "What about Duncan Papadopoulos?" I offered. "He's an outsider who everyone is automatically suspicious of. Maybe that's a cliché for a reason."

"Making three people disappear takes effort. Duncan's stalking of Aviva aside, what would his endgame be? A few thousand dollars for the homeless? Doesn't seem worth it."

"I question Aviva's stalking claim. The Schubert sisters think Duncan is innocuous, and we didn't sense an aggressive side to him either."

"Why would Aviva lie? We saw the hatchback this morning, circling her drive."

The speed and size of the rain increased, so I dashed under the pavilion. Levi lifted his boots off the bench to make room for me.

"But we didn't see the driver." I sat down. "Even if it was Duncan, several things could explain his actions. He could have a poor sense of direction, got lost running errands, and wheeled around on her drive."

"And Aviva's fear? Just award-worthy acting?"

"Aviva might believe Duncan is a stalker, but that doesn't make it true. In a small town, it seems near impossible to avoid anyone. Perhaps Aviva's anxiety over her husband's disappearance has manifested itself in other ways. She sees the hatchback around town and fears someone is after her."

Levi nodded. "That might explain her Arbor Day shellacking of Gunderson. Maybe she's stressed—about Fredrich's disappearance, about the election—and imagines these enemies."

"I think you were right about simplifying our theory. Everything we've learned today takes us back to money."

"Money, money, money." Levi flicked his thumb across his fingertips. "Epic fraud all centered on money laundering."

"Money laundering?"

He leaned forward. "It would explain the pattern of small amounts of money. The stuff at the construction site, a little federal money here, a police development grant there. Those small amounts add up to a sizeable sum."

"Doesn't that money need to be… washed? Where would that happen?"

"In legitimate businesses where cash flows in and out. Like the café."

I smacked my hand on the picnic table. "The Cherry Blossom? Now, c'mon, you know Jenny—"

"Not Jenny, Javi. He ran a café, a business he had no experience in and where no one ate. He also managed the town's commercial real estate. Lots of flowin' money there."

"The scale of what you're suggesting requires more than just Javi. Basically, everyone in town would have to be a criminal." I chuckled nervously. "How do you know about this stuff, anyway?"

"My show, of course."

"Your tween detective show tackled money laundering?"

"Season 3, episode 3, 'Rub-A-Dub-Dub, Dirty Money in My Tub.'" Levi's gaze then drifted behind me. He turned ashen, and he gripped the tabletop.

"I told y'all to lie low."

I spun toward Chief Gunderson's voice. His expression was vacant, his fists balled, the rain melting the gel that made his hair so mannequin-stiff.

I glanced nervously at Levi. "We were waiting out the rain, and then I was coming to see you. I want to fly home tonight."

Gunderson's body snapped like he'd awakened from a dream. "Why were y'all talking to that nosy reporter? What did she say about me?" He swatted the air with his meaty hands. "No matter, it's all lies." He marched toward me, but then spun to the wall that separated us from the river.

"She… she said nothing," I said. "I was buying flowers for my sister. Have you… have you seen Jenny recently?"

"I can't go to prison. I love this town; I should be running it." His voice had a whimpering quality. "They won't understand; they won't get why I did it."

"Who won't understand, chief? What did you do?"

"The Rangers. They'll find out what happened, what I did to Ernst. It'll be over for me."

I swallowed. "What… did you do to Fredrich Ernst?"

Gunderson's eyes locked on me. I thought he was going to charge. Instead, he swiveled and paced beside the wall. "He didn't love this town, understand that. We were just another rung on his political ladder. He'd eventually smash our face in when he needed that next step."

"Are you talking about the mayoral race?" Levi asked. "The one you were a candidate for?"

"See? I knew that reporter shot her mouth off." Gunderson tugged at his wet hair, which spiked in large tufts. "Ernst, he was a nobody congressman, your typical East Coast liberal. But he wanted a higher office, and he knew he had to broaden his voter base."

I looked again at Levi. Were we supposed to keep him talking? Did we have an exit strategy? "So, he returned to Texas? Ran for mayor?"

Gunderson spread his hands as if unveiling a billboard. "The favorite son of Bluebonnet Hills returns to reverse its financial fortunes."

"That script practically writes itself," Levi muttered under his breath. "I'd kill for that part."

I swatted his hand and growled. "Probably not the best word choice."

But Gunderson wasn't paying attention. "Ernst ran his campaign on growing small businesses and reforming education. Everything he voted against in Congress. All part of the rebrand, and I guess an attempt to rehabilitate his marriage."

"He and Aviva were having issues?"

"I guess you could say that." He flashed his capped teeth. "You can't run for president when your loving wife is having an affair. Moving Aviva here didn't end that."

"The affair continued? Long distance?" I asked.

Gunderson shook his head. "The dude moved here."

"Here? As in Bluebonnet Hills here?" Levi and I were mirror images, our eyes round, mouths slightly agape. "Wait a second, was Aviva having an affair with… with Duncan Papadopoulos?"

Levi gave a low whistle. "I guess the reverend has more flavor than just vanilla."

Chapter 17

Gunderson's cell phone rang from inside his shorts. He grabbed the fabric outside the pocket, fumbling to silence the ringer. It was hard to hear through the rain, but his ringtone sounded like the theme from *Bonanza*.

I asked, "Chief, so I understand, when did you decide to make Fredrich Ernst, uh, disappear?"

"Getting elected was easy for him, but then he had to actually govern. The revitalization didn't move as quickly as he'd hoped, even with Javi Zepeda cutting corners. He needed a problem to solve, so he created one. And blamed me for it."

"You mean the crime surge, and the rumor you fudged the crime stats?" Levi asked.

"Why would I do that?" Gunderson smacked his forehead. "Ernst knew I wouldn't go along with the plan, so he bribed my own people. And they came cheap. Throw some money and a trumped-up commendation at Deputy Perkins and suddenly we have ourselves a crime spree. And when that nosy Schubert twin started asking questions, Ernst dumped it all on me."

I nodded. "I understand why that would upset you."

"And Aviva wasn't much better. She knew what Ernst was doing, and she planned to continue with his work."

Aviva said she wanted to fulfill her husband's legacy. Perhaps this was what she meant. Gunderson had referred to her in the past tense. I guessed he had also made her disappear.

I scraped my feet against the ground. "What about Javi? Did you…?"

Gunderson sighed. "Javi followed the plan for a while; he and Ernst go way back. But his conscience eventually got the better of him. He came to me, and I told him to leave town and let me figure this out."

My shoulders stiffened. "Javi can help you then. Have him explain all this to the Texas Rangers."

"It's too late for that. I can't go to prison." His pacing resumed. "I'm too pretty for prison. Y'all have to tell them."

"Sure… we can tell them," I said. "But, why can't you tell them? Where will you be?"

Gunderson's musical shorts went off again.

Bum-badabum-badadadadabum-Bo-nan-za. Despite the tense situation, it was impossible not to sing that to myself. Levi's finger tapping showed he was doing the same.

The chief dug out his phone and held it to his ear. "Yeah?" He twisted away from us.

I spoke in a hoarse whisper. "Let's get out of here. Gunderson is not stable."

Levi turned toward the chief. "We could run for it, but have you seen the size of his calf muscles? He'd catch at least one of us. And my legs are longer than yours."

Gunderson effortlessly leapt onto the rock wall that bordered the river. The spectacle was shocking, as if something nonhuman was storming the castle. He released the grip on his phone, which ricocheted off the wall and disappeared. He wrapped his fingers around his revolver, glistening matte black with silver highlights.

I rose from my seat. "He's going to…" I thought he was going to turn the gun on himself. Instead, he aimed it at us.

Something whizzed past my ear. Reflexively, I swatted the air to fend off any flying insects. The popping that followed and the exploding river rocks near Gunderson indicated the sound was not angry hornets.

"Get down!" Levi lunged across the picnic table and pushed me off the bench. I fell squarely on my shoulder, and my foot caught on the table's base and twisted.

A second shot fired, this one from Gunderson's direction. The bullet drove past us, into the surrounding hills. Levi rolled off the tabletop and onto the cement pad with a grunt. I untangled my foot from the bench and then crawled around near him.

A crack and thump signaled the third shot from the hills, which pinged off the ground near us. My chest tightened, my brow hot with sweat.

Images flashed through my head. I was back in Seattle, in the ICU. The patient, her husband, the gun, her eyes. I was hungry for air, losing control.

1-2-3. Breathe.

1-2-3. This isn't working.

1-2-3. I'm going to die.

"Tanaka-san? Tanaka-san?" Levi. "Focus here, look at me. You're okay."

I blinked. The blackness faded, and Levi's face came into focus. 1-2-3. 1-2-3. The ringing in my ears subsided. The rain had stopped. I glanced at the rock wall, but there was no sign of Gunderson. I patted myself down to check for holes.

Levi's hair was disheveled, his cheek bruised from lunging and rolling. "Stay there. Catch your breath first."

I was gorging on oxygen like it was prime rib at an all-you-can-eat buffet. "What just happened?"

Levi held a hand over his eyes like a visor, peering into the hills. "Someone wanted us dead, or Gunderson dead, or all of us dead."

"I… I need to find Jenny." I pushed myself up, losing to gravity and plopping down.

"Stay down. We'll find Jenny, but you need to stop and breathe first."

The sounds of crunching gravel grew faster and louder behind me. I turned and stared at Duncan Papadopoulos's hiking boots, scrubbed and polished to a shiny clean. His hands trembled slightly as he gripped the rifle, its polished wood stock adding to his catalog-ready appearance. The thin smile he offered me triggered the reality that he was not just modeling outdoor menswear but had shot a police chief.

"Are you hurt?" Duncan glided past us, rifle still raised, and pointed it over the rock wall where I'd last seen Gunderson.

I rubbed the knot bulging in my forehead. "I'm fine." It was a difficult situation to process. Why did Aviva Ernst's lover just shoot Gunderson, and were we the next targets? The fact he probably wasn't a reverend didn't matter at this point.

Levi dusted the dirt and gravel off his jeans, but he stayed fixed on Duncan. He was asking the same questions.

"Sorry I'm late." Duncan lowered his rifle, still watching the river. "I lost track of you when you took the Segways here."

Was the entire town following us? That question also seemed irrelevant.

"We should leave. We're pretty exposed out here." He dropped the rifle to his side and offered me a hand to help me stand. I flinched. The pungent smell of his smoky orange-scented cologne made me dizzy. "Your sister's safe. I'll take you to her."

Still confused by his motives, I used the picnic table to pull myself up. I wobbled on my feet like a cruise ship passenger. "You have Jenny? Why?"

"To protect her." Duncan's shoulder slumped. "Sorry, my adrenaline is still pumping, and you don't know who I am."

"Your Aviva Ernst's man candy," Levi said, ever so tactfully.

"Aviva's…?" Duncan's eyebrows knitted in confusion.

"Her lover," I clarified.

"Lover? Who told you that? She's… almost my mom's age."

The response made me chuckle. "Gunderson said you and Aviva were having an affair; that's why you're in Bluebonnet Hills."

Duncan shook his head slowly, absorbing the information. "I'm a fed, special agent with the Department of Treasury. I'm here to uncover fraud." He pointed his thumb behind him. "That call that Gunderson just received? It was the order to take you out."

"Take us out?" Levi asked.

Duncan sighed. "You two have stepped into more sh—" He stopped to compose himself. "I'll explain on the way. Let's go meet Jenny."

I fished my phone from my pocket, impressed that the screen was unblemished. "I've been trying to reach her. Does she have her phone?"

Duncan focused on the phone in my outstretched hand. "I asked her to turn that off, and I recommend you both do the same. We're not sure how many of the local police are compromised. You're probably being tracked by GPS."

Recalling what Gunderson had said about Deputy Perkins being bribed, I powered my phone off. Levi did the same.

Duncan motioned toward the path we had traveled to the river. "Let's move out. I've got your sister's car." He spun around, not waiting for a response.

"Where are you taking us?" We passed the Segways and hiked back the way we'd driven in.

Duncan's eyes darted up to the trees and brush. "The construction site for the museum. We'll stay there until I'm authorized to move you. Jenny's already there; a colleague is with her."

Levi and I stumbled and bumbled behind, eventually finding our way to the road and my sister's lime green hatchback.

Duncan opened the passenger-side door and moved the seat forward. "Try to hunch down. We might be followed." He glanced over his shoulder and tightened his grip on the rifle's barrel.

"Gunderson?" I asked him. "Is he...?"

"You don't have to worry about him."

I climbed into the back seat and scrunched behind the driver's seat. Duncan slid the passenger seat forward to allow Levi more room to fold his legs and hunch down.

"Treasury Department? So, this *was* all about money?" I asked Duncan when he'd settled into his seat.

He cranked the ignition and adjusted his mirrors. "Fredrich Ernst has been on our radar for a while, beginning with some suspicious transactions in his congressional campaign. He moved here to expand his criminal activities." He sped onto the street in the direction of the construction site. "Sounds like you figured that out already."

"Not really," I said. "We have some theories but aren't clear on how everything fits together."

"I'll tell you what I can. What all have you found so far?"

"Money in the wall at the construction site," Levi said. "We thought you put it there, that you were stealing the money to help the homeless."

"Solid theory. And good to know my undercover performance had some credibility." He paused. "Have you found any leads on Javi?"

"We think he's dead," I said. "He wanted to confess something, perhaps be a whistleblower."

"You'll be relieved to know that Javi is hiding out. He'll be the star witness at the trial."

"We saw you at Aviva's house," I said. "Have you been following us all day?"

"When I could keep up." There was a lightness in his tone. "I overheard your conversation at breakfast about visiting the construction site. Figured you might get yourself into trouble."

"You figured right," Levi said.

"Suppose you also found the blankets, the food items?"

My knees pushed against the seat when the car hit a bump. "Odessa Schubert has a theory that Javi's nephew was facilitating an illegal scheme involving immigration."

"She's a sharp reporter. But Gunderson was the mastermind there. Tito was just the muscle; he doesn't have the brains to create that level of operation."

"But Gunderson did?" I asked.

Duncan snickered. "Gunderson had the law enforcement know-how. The construction site was his new location. He'd just moved the operation from an abandoned gas station. Levi, you arriving here was an unlucky coincidence for him."

"My sister… her recruitment to Bluebonnet Hills seems related to all this. But, is she directly involved with any of these activities?"

I could see some of Duncan's profile when he glanced down. "Jenny's a victim of circumstance, for sure. But she's here to divert suspicion, make people believe this town is roaring to life. Whatever goes down here, your sister is in the clear."

That gave me some comfort.

Our semi-smooth car ride got bumpier when we hit the gravel road to the construction site. Duncan pulled the car behind the building and grabbed his rifle from the front seat. I noticed there were no steps leading up to the back door. The migrants I'd encountered must have leapt to the ground before they ran off.

"Jenny's inside. Go on ahead," Duncan said.

Levi and I ran to the front of the building and bounded up the steps. The interior looked the same, dark, putrid smelling, the money packed into the drywall.

"Hello? Jenny?!" I swiveled to Levi, my heart beating hard. "Where is she?"

Levi ran to the smaller room. "Over here. Where's your flashlight?"

I fumbled with my phone, realizing I'd turned it off. "It'll take me a second...."

Levi advanced into the room's darkness, and I could hear muffled sounds coming from the corner. Jenny sat in a metal chair, her arms bound behind her, her mouth gagged with duct tape.

I dropped my phone. "Jenny." I advanced toward her, but an arm pulled me into the tip of a rifle.

"Sorry, man," Duncan said. "Nothing personal."

It seemed kind of personal.

Levi yelped when a pistol jabbed into his upper back. He raised his hands slowly.

"Stay still, Mr. Blue." Aviva Ernst yanked Levi's phone from his pocket and then tossed it on the floor.

Chapter 18

"**W**ELL, I SHOULD HAVE SEEN THIS COMING,**"** Levi said, gun to his head. "Pretend mayor pretends to disappear. Hats off to you, m'lady."

"Please," Aviva said. "You fell for a clichéd 'woman in peril' story. I'm actually embarrassed for you."

Jenny's head slumped forward, her body slack in the chair. She made an occasional moan, but the overall lethargy suggested she'd been drugged, or worn out from the fight.

Duncan's free hand nudged the small of my back, willing me toward my sister. He spun another metal chair around. "Sit down, Sho."

I turned and folded my arms. "What did you do to her?"

Duncan responded by pressing his fist into my gut, causing me to flop into the seat. He rested his rifle against the wall.

"Just a mild sedative," Aviva said. "Your sister has a bite to her. Quite literally."

Duncan rubbed the arm of his long sleeve, presumably from the bite Jenny had given him. Good.

"Is all of this necessary? If you and your lover want to swindle the town and run off with its money, that's your business. We don't care, and Jenny's not a part in this."

Duncan muttered, "I already told you, we're not together."

He'd also told us he was a fed. Right before he told us he was a reverend. Duncan grabbed a roll of duct tape from somewhere on the floor and wrapped it around my arms and the chair rails.

"Of course she's a part of this," Aviva spoke in a mocking tone. "A daffy second-generation Japanese American who brings her fusion cuisine to li'l ol' Bluebonnet Hills?" She shoved Levi toward another empty chair. "She legitimatized the lie. And she played her part to perfection."

Finished with duct-taping my arms to the chair rails, Duncan wrapped tape across my chest and to the back of the chair. I recalled the *Bluebonnet Bee* feature about Jenny and the café. It seemed Levi's theory was correct, and my sister had helped distract from all the money crimes. All this time, she was being used. The realization she'd been plucked out of culinary school to be the town token made my skin prick and my fists clench.

Duncan moved to the second chair. He was several inches shorter than Levi, a difference he seemed to notice. "Don't be a hero, Levi. This isn't a TV show."

Levi snorted and perched in the chair, flopping his arms on the rails to assist Duncan.

"So, was this the plan all along?" Levi asked. "You and Fredrich leave Jersey to swindle a small town? Yawn, talk about cliché."

Aviva cocked her head and gave a thin smile. "Is this where I'm supposed to deliver a long-winded monologue about why I did it?"

"We are in the third act."

"And it's your curtain call, Mr. Blue." Aviva steadied her hold of the pistol.

Duncan ripped a long piece of tape, breaking the tension. "Enough with the dramatics. It's like a telenovela in here." He wrapped the tape across Levi's chest. "We'll be gone in a few hours. Just sit here and keep the quips to yourself."

The commotion roused Jenny. She shifted in her chair and her murmurs grew louder. I twisted my neck, but my chest was constrained by the chair. "It'll all be okay," I said to her.

"I'll get her some water," Duncan said, slipping into the other room.

"So, the revitalization of Bluebonnet Hills?" I asked Aviva. "That was an empty campaign promise to get Fredrich elected mayor? He was already a US congressman. I don't understand."

Aviva stepped closer to me, and I could see the tightness in her face. "Fredrich never pandered for votes. The Ernst family founded this Hill Country hell. His hope for a revitalization was sincere, one of his more disagreeable character traits."

"Then what was the point!?"

"It's not obvious? You think too much, Mr. Tanaka."

It wasn't the first time someone had accused me of that today. Surprisingly, Levi had the self-control and good sense not to yell out, *Toldja.*

Aviva said, "This was all about money. Lots and lots of money. It's the only motivation one needs."

Duncan returned with the water, causing Jenny to jerk her chair away. "I'm sorry about all this, Jen," he said softly. He raised his hand to the tape across her mouth. "This will hurt. Sorry about that too."

He peeled the tape away, and I winced at the sound of my sister's whimpers. Duncan held a plastic straw to her lips, and she began to drink.

After several gulps of water, she pulled away from the straw. "I have a question," she said to Aviva. Her voice was soft but strong.

Aviva sighed heavily but inched forward.

"When you recruited me, you said I was exactly what this town needed."

"And you were, sweetheart. Just what I needed. And what you needed too. You profited from the exposure; a fluff news article, your face plastered on all the new marketing materials. You can play victim with the boys, but not with me."

And then my sister unleashed a string of expletives that made me both blush and smile. I'd have given her a fist pump if I wasn't duct-taped to a chair. When she was finished, Jenny opened her mouth for more water, as she was parched after her longshoreman-inspired broadside.

"Lovely," Aviva said flatly. And then to Duncan: "We need to separate everyone. Keep the boys here, but tape the backs of their chairs together. Move Jenny into the other room and cut a fresh gag for that dainty mouth."

"Aviva, this wasn't—"

"—wasn't the plan?" She wagged her pistol. "Don't lecture me on plans, *Reverend.* Take your own advice and keep the quips to yourself."

Duncan hesitated before lifting the chair from the floor. Jenny yelled and tried to kick her feet out, but the tape had her strapped down. Levi and I both rose from our chairs, but our own body weight knocked us down.

"Don't hurt her!" I said.

"You're in control of that, Mr. Tanaka," Aviva said.

"You won't get away with this," Levi said.

Aviva released a bark of laughter. "Won't I? This isn't an episode of *Scooby Doo*, Mr. Blue, and you're past your prime for the role of the meddling kid."

DARKNESS LEAKED THROUGH THE WINDOWS and door of the construction site. Duncan had removed the food cans and bottles, but the mats and afghans, still reeking of body odor, remained. Mouth breathing helped dissipate my reflex to vomit. From the other room, Jenny moaned occasionally as she drifted in and out of consciousness. Levi and I sat back-to-back, our chairs taped together. Outside, a croaking sound echoed from all directions.

"What's that noise?" I asked. It sounded like a million cans of soda exploding all at once.

"Cicadas, it's a mating sound." Levi shifted in his chair, his legs likely cramping. "They'll be shriveled up and glued to the building tomorrow morning."

Not the most hopeful imagery for our current situation. Once everyone was repositioned, Duncan and Aviva left. We heard them pad down the steps and murmurs of an indistinct conversation. Then nothing. No slamming car doors or engines running. The anticipation of them bursting through the door to shoot us kept me from relaxing.

"I'm going to count us down," Levi said. "On three, try to stand up and push your arms out. The impact should break the tape."

I sucked in a breath. "Is this a technique you learned from the show?"

"Not exactly. After my legitimate acting gigs dried up, I was hired as an actor for a self-defense class. I got tied up and kneed and punched pretty regularly." The chairs shimmied as Levi centered himself. "Ready? One. Two. Three."

My shoes barely touched the ground, so I had to depend on core strength to stand. But Levi was taller and heavier, and I had no core strength, so I toppled back instead of forward. Our chairs landed with a thud, my wrists burning from the duct tape.

"Sorry. I didn't account for our weight differences," Levi said. "You okay?"

"Yeah, let me catch my breath before we try again." I closed my eyes and willed the burning sensations to fade. My mind flooded with questions about what was happening in Bluebonnet Hills, but listening to Aviva earlier made me aware of how shamefully I'd behaved since I'd arrived in this town. "I'm a jerk," I announced.

"I'm listening," Levi said.

"Aviva's behavior this evening, the way she denigrated the town, the people here. It was ugly. And that's how I've been acting toward Jenny. She called me a snob the other day. I don't mean to be, but I suppose she's right."

"She's perceptive," Levi said. "And smart and capable. Just because they're not your choices doesn't make them wrong."

I nodded. "My recent track record for making excellent choices has been spotty. And that's being generous."

"Stop torturing yourself over that thing with Tito Ramirez. You were anxious, looking for some relief. Try to remember you're human."

"Soliciting drugs from Tito was only the most recent of my poor choices. I'm visiting Jenny because my hospital put me on administrative leave. There's nothing waiting for me in Seattle. Well, junk mail, but that's not as exciting as it sounds."

"The drug use, is that why you're on leave?"

"My psychiatrist alleges I have post-traumatic stress. The drug abuse relates more to how I'm processing everything."

"You don't have to tell me, but what caused the trauma?"

I'd replayed the incident a million times, yet I struggled with where to begin. "Two months ago, I attended a patient after a car accident. She was fleeing her abusive ex-husband and smacked into an eighteen-wheeler coming from the other direction."

"Did she survive?"

"She was in critical condition, but we were optimistic. Until the ex-husband appeared to finish the job. With a gun." I swallowed. "I'll never forget the look in the patient's eyes when he aimed it at her."

"Fear?"

"Relief." I pursed my lips. "She'd been living in fear for so long that knowing the end seemed somehow liberating."

"And was that the end?"

"No. I threw myself on top of her like some human blanket."

"You shielded her? That was courageous. Did you get shot?"

I shook my head and laughed. "It was a toy. Doofus brought a toy gun into the ICU."

"But you didn't know it was a toy. I understand why the hospital wants you to talk to someone."

"When the realization hit that I had tackled a critical patient, I snapped. I lunged for the ex-husband and then literally pistol-whipped him."

"Ha, that's amazing."

"But once reality set in, when I realized I'd lost control… that's when the prescription drug abuse began. I didn't feel safe at work. Even the lurch between elevator floors made me jumpy. I manipulated colleagues for additional prescriptions, deluded myself that I could self-monitor my intake. I sacrificed my personal life and family time to excel at my job. Now I have nothing."

"I knew you had a tortured backstory. Is that why you're in Bluebonnet Hills? To escape?"

"Jenny has this knack for making the monumental appear inconsequential. You get sucked into her enthusiasm bubble, and it puts things into perspective."

"You should tell her what's happening in your life."

"I want to apologize to you, too, for making light of the fan museum. I thought you were driven by ego, but I understand your connection to this place."

"Being here keeps my dad's spirit alive."

"Obviously, I don't watch a lot of TV, but was he in anything I might have seen?"

"He did mostly period dramas."

"I love those, actually."

"Remember that show about the sexy lifeguards? They were always running along the beach in slow motion?"

"He was in that?"

"He was in an earlier version. They actually ripped off that opening shot from my dad's show."

"This was a period drama?"

"It was set on a beach during the 1920s Jazz Age. *Seaside Razzamatazz.* Alas, that slow-mo shot wasn't so sexy with everyone wearing knitted wool swim dresses and flowered caps."

"Levi?"

"Yeah, bud?"

"If we make it out of this alive, you're not allowed to speak to me. Ever again."

"You're the boss, boss."

The croaking symphony outside continued, sounding like dozens of vibrating speakers all jacked up at once.

"How old was your dad?" I asked. "When he passed?"

"Fifty-six."

"That is young."

He gave a soft chuckle. "That's even what they call the disease, young-onset dementia. Of course, twenty-five years ago, they diagnosed my dad as quirky. As the disease progressed, he got upgraded to nutty, and finally to stark raving mad. It must be a painful disease to experience because it's pure torture to watch. Have you heard of it?"

I had. It was an uncommon form of dementia, but shared the same progressively worsening effects as all forms of the disease. "Adjusting to dementia is also hard on the families. I've seen that firsthand. Lots of stress, lots of challenges."

"Dad didn't know what was happening. Nobody did. I was a kid; he just always seemed like my dad. And this form of dementia can be hereditary." His voice grew softer. "Lately, I've been jumbling things up in my head, losing my words." He gave another chuckle. "More than I usually do."

"That could be related to stress or many other factors. Have you seen a specialist?"

"I'm not ready to know yet. Too many madcap adventures to have."

"Is that why you're in Bluebonnet Hills? Madcap and mayhem?"

"And hijinks and shenanigans. Hollywood never felt like home. But this is a great place to tackle my bucket list."

"Your bucket list? You're too young for one of those."

"I grew up on a soundstage. My closest friends were my agent and a prop master. The more success I experienced, the more friends I collected. Then the show was cancelled, and all those so-called friends cancelled me. I missed out on a lot."

I stared into the blackness of the room. "If I planned, I convinced myself that I'd never fail. This weekend made me realize that I've been missing out too. I don't even know what I want anymore."

"Great, you get a bucket list, too," Levi said. "What should we do first?"

"Staying alive would be a nice. Any more ideas?" I asked.

"We could tip these chairs over and inch our way to freedom.

Barbara Lou Sinclair is probably patrolling the neighborhood. She'll call for help. After she maces us."

"Solid plan, but I don't want to leave Jenny."

"Agreed. You think they'll come back here?"

"Yes. Duncan appeared uneasy with everything, and he expressed concern for Jenny. Perhaps he can be persuaded with logic."

"You mean Reverend Yanni? How's he going to help? Compose some New Agey music for our escape scene?"

Something clicked in my head. "What did you say?"

"Maybe his mellow keyboard stylings will lull Aviva into a coma. If that doesn't knock her flat, that pungent cologne he wears will."

I vaguely remembered; we were at the flower shop. "What did Abilene tell us? About Javi's family?"

"Uh… Tito's his nephew. And, he's divorced, has a son he doesn't mention a lot…."

"Calista. His wife's name is Calista. Is that Greek?"

"Seems like it should be."

"Calista Papadopoulos."

"That's definitely Greek."

"He used his mother's maiden name. Of course."

"Who?"

"You're brilliant, Levi. Yanni. That's Duncan's first name. XYZ Construction. It's not a generic company name. XYZ stands for Xavier and Yanni Zepeda."

As if on cue, the door opened and Duncan, or Yanni, stepped inside. He held a flashlight and something metallic. When he raised it, I could clearly make out a utility knife.

Chapter 19

DUNCAN WAVED THE FLASHLIGHT into the room where Jenny was tied up. I opened my mouth to shout, but he flicked the light directly into my eyes. I turned, blinking wildly, but the light grew brighter as he moved toward us. Levi bucked, our chairs moving closer to the wall.

"Relax, I'm cutting you loose." Duncan crouched down and worked the utility knife through the tape around my legs.

"Are you letting us go?" I asked.

Duncan focused silently on his work.

"I know who you are, Yanni Zepeda." I said. "Javi is your father."

The cutting stopped. "I knew I'd slipped up with that whole name thing at breakfast. Guess I make for a lousy criminal."

"Stealing money from small business owners? You're doing okay in the criminal department," Levi said.

When Duncan looked up, the glow from the flashlight revealed his hollow cheeks. "For what it's worth, I care about Jenny. I want the café to be successful. I didn't steal much from her. What I took, I put back. Dad was furious, said all a family business did was cost him money."

"Then what was the point?" I asked. "Surely, there are easier ways to make money than posing as the town reverend. Not to mention the time investment in these people's businesses, in their lives."

Duncan scooted to work on my other leg. "Dad and Fredrich Ernst came up with the reverend story. I have a theology degree, just didn't think I'd use it like this. It was all temporary, to get me here to help Dad."

I stretched my legs out into the darkness. "I don't understand. Help your dad do what? Defraud the town?"

"Dad wanted to teach me the construction business. The *legitimate* business. The fraud with Levi's museum, the seven percent cash discount, all schemes my dad cooked up. But this wasn't about greed."

"Your father spent most of his life in Bluebonnet Hills. Why ruin his business, betray the people he's known for decades?"

"Dad is overly idealistic; it's his best and his worst quality. His latest plan was to establish a trade school for new migrants. He wanted to teach them the construction business, build up their skills, give them an opportunity."

"That's an admirable goal," I said. "But why mastermind an immigration scheme to accomplish it?"

Duncan rose from his knees to shake the knife at me. "I told you, that was Gunderson's operation. It disgusted my dad. He came here legally, but he understood why others couldn't—and the horrific conditions they could be subjected to all based on someone's empty promise." He sawed through the tape around my arm too quickly for my comfort.

"I understand," Levi said. "Your dad was trying to do something good. Sounds like he saw himself as a kind of Robin Hood."

"He felt horrible about deceiving his friends here." Duncan cut the last of my tape away and moved on to Levi. "But he sacrificed a lot for this town, his family, his health. No excuses; he made a mistake. But he did a lot of good here, too. But all that will be erased when his deceptions are revealed."

I rubbed my tender wrists. I stole drugs to benefit myself, while Javi stole money to empower people. Neither of us felt we should be judged solely for that choice, yet the comparison between us made me realize how I'd lost control. "You said your father sacrificed his health for Bluebonnet Hills. Was he sick?"

"He said there was asbestos in his lungs, from all the construction sites he'd worked on."

I closed my eyes, sorry my theory about Javi having mesothelioma was probably true. "Did he seek treatment?"

Duncan moved from Levi's feet to his hands. "Fredrich kept encouraging him to fight, and offered to pay for any treatments he needed."

"But Javi refused?"

"Actually, his good sense trumped his everyday stubbornness. He agreed to this experimental treatment, found a private hospital in Houston. Then Fredrich disappeared."

Levi stretched his legs and grunted. "And so Fredrich's money disappeared too?"

Duncan retracted the knife and shoved it in his back pocket. "I suggested we use the stolen money, but he wouldn't consider it. His conscience finally kicked in. He said to forget it, but, I mean... he's my dad."

"You couldn't forget about it." Levi nodded. "You went to Aviva, didn't you? Asked her for the money?"

Duncan stood and took a deep breath. "She avoided me. I finally approached her at home. She flipped out, demanded medical documentation." He shook his head in disbelief. "He and Dad were practically brothers. I said she was ignoring Fredrich's wishes, and it wasn't like she didn't have the money."

When I'd visited Aviva, she'd also requested my medical documentation. She'd told the truth about her confrontation with Duncan, but lied about the topic of conversation. "Does Aviva know you're Javi's son?"

"Only Fredrich. And Tito, of course. Dad said he had enemies who might exploit the family connection, that's why he enlisted Fredrich for the fake reverend help. I visited Aviva as the saintly Reverend Papadopoulos." He gave himself a self-congratulatory smile, and I wondered how naïve Duncan truly was.

"What did your father say after you spoke to Aviva?" I asked.

"I didn't tell him. He'd freak. Besides, he was busy feuding with Gunderson over this immigration scheme."

"I thought Javi wasn't part of that."

Duncan's jaw clenched, and he started to pace. "Gunderson wanted to use these sites for the migrants he brought in. Dad refused, but Gunderson knew about the construction fraud. He threatened to expose Dad if he didn't cooperate."

"That's pretty risky on Gunderson's part," I said. "Your father could have exposed him too."

Duncan stopped pacing. "And that became his new plan. Like I said before, his conscience returned. He said the risks to his family weren't worth it, and it was time he confessed his sins to the people he hurt." He raised a hand to Levi.

"Your dad reached out to me," Levi said. "But he never showed up at our meeting."

"I guess he couldn't before he left town. He told me to stay here, that my disappearance would link us. After two months, he said to take the remaining money, rent a car, and drive to St. Augustine. He'd find me there."

"But your father didn't make it," I said.

Duncan gave a short laugh. "Didn't you get a postcard?"

I tilted my head to one side, wondering if this was the setup or the punchline. Clearly, Duncan believed his father was alive. "Who told you to take out Gunderson? Was it Javi?"

Duncan stared at the ground. "Aviva called me, warning me. She knew I'd been stealing from people, but that Gunderson was calling the Texas Rangers to investigate." He looked up, his eyes watery, his voice low. "He was an absent father, always promising his next investment would be 'the one.' And we'd be a family again. Remember that folk song? 'Cat's in the Cradle'? That was our relationship. Still, he loved me. And I wouldn't let Gunderson ruin my dad's reputation."

The glow of headlights backlit Duncan, painting his skin gray, illuminating his gaunt features. My body shook from the vibrations of whatever was attached to those headlights. I guessed a large truck.

"What's that?" Levi asked.

I jumped when the truck rolled to a screech and stopped. It idled outside, the vibrations working through my body.

"This wasn't… you weren't part of the plan," Duncan said. He grappled with the retractable knife and a key from his pocket. "Get Jenny and get out of here. That key unlocks the back door. Run through the empty field behind us. You'll eventually find the main road."

Levi grabbed the knife and dashed to Jenny.

"Duncan, you're in as much danger as we are. Aviva knows who you are."

"She doesn't. Fredrich wouldn't tell her." He cocked his head toward the wall of money. "I'll be all right."

"What about Tito? Perhaps he told Aviva who you are."

Duncan shook his head. "He's family."

The door to the building burst open. I blinked into the darkness, adjusting to the outline in the doorway. Duncan looked too. And gasped.

Chief Tex Gunderson, dressed in a polo shirt—collar popped—and cargo shorts, glided into the room. He aimed his Glock at me with one hand and held a black duffel bag with the other.

"Surprised to see me, little man?"

Chapter 20

GUNDERSON DROPPED THE DUFFEL BAG and strutted toward Levi. "I'll take that." He reached for the knife Levi was using to cut Jenny free.

Levi glanced from the knife to Gunderson's pistol, considering his options. Realizing he'd literally brought a knife to a gunfight, Levi retracted the blade and slapped the plastic into Gunderson's outstretched hand and stood in front of Jenny.

Gunderson smiled slyly and kicked the duffel bag to the center of the room. "Fill it up," he said to Duncan.

Duncan rubbed his neck. "Fill what up?"

"Dumb truly is your color; it brings out your eyes." The glint from Gunderson's capped teeth offered better visibility than the flashlight. "Gimme some of that money you've been squirreling away."

Duncan stared down. Like Levi, he considered his options. Also like Levi, he realized the lack of options and gripped the bag.

"Aviva said we could go," I said. "Can you cut my sister loose?"

Gunderson squinted at me. "She looks comfy cozy to me."

I eyed Levi, who continued to guard Jenny. He had the back door key, and we couldn't overpower Gunderson and escape through the front. Besides, I didn't know what was waiting for us outside. I turned toward the afghans and mats piled in the corner. "The temperature is dropping. At least give her something warm." I pinched the yarn of a blanket with my fingers, looking for one with the least offensive odor and hoping a rusty can top might fall out. That would be some weapon.

"That one there has cross stitch on it." Gunderson pointed his pistol at the rainbow-colored afghan I was subjecting to the smell test. "That way you don't have to change the yarn colors."

"Um, okay…" I recalled that Gunderson crocheted as a hobby. Levi took the blanket from me and laid it over my sister's lap.

Gunderson puffed out his chest. "My work's gotten a lot better since that one. I figure my career in law enforcement is over, so I might open a craft store. Already got a name for it—Yarnspiration."

It took a lot of effort not to roll my eyes.

Aviva poked her head inside the door. "Everything all right in here, babe?"

Babe? Who was the babe?

Gunderson turned to her and smiled. "I was just yakking about Yarnspiration."

Aviva crossed to him and danced her fingers up his spine

and over his shoulder. She lightly tugged his earlobe and then whispered, "Did you buy the tickets?"

Gunderson's lips scrunched. "I had to adjust the plan, darlin'. I couldn't exactly pop home for my passport. We'll drive across the border tonight and regroup. Reverend Papadopoulos is packing us a little mad money for the road."

Aviva pulled away and gave a playful pout. "Mexico? Pooh. Remember who's in charge here, chief. Multiple changes to the plan didn't work out for my *dear* Freddy."

Gunderson shrugged as if he'd heard that threat before.

Duncan dropped a stack of cash into the duffel bag. "What's going on here, Aviva? You told me to drop Tex in the river."

"Clearly, you failed," she said with a laugh. "Tex had to leave town before the pressure mounted to find my body. A second missing mayor would make national news, and we all couldn't disappear at once. We needed to scare off Scooby and Shaggy here, so they became witnesses to his murder."

"Were you going to tell me... any of this?" Duncan grasped a fistful of his hair. "If you were planning on witnesses, you were planning to frame me for murder."

Aviva released an exasperated sigh. "An additional insurance policy in case the plan wasn't executed. Which it wasn't." She pointed to Jenny. "She wasn't part of the plan either."

"I panicked." Duncan kicked the duffel bag toward Gunderson. "She confronted me about the way I'd been handling her finances."

"Panic made you sloppy." Aviva continued running her fingers up Gunderson's bicep. "Thankfully, Tex was here to clean everything up. Finally, a man who listens to me and takes action." She gazed at the floor and smiled. "Do you hear that, Freddy, my love?"

Aviva stomped her heel twice into the concrete floor.

And my stomach lurched at the realization of where Fredrich Ernst's body had probably been disposed.

Gunderson said to Duncan, "Help me drag these two outside. Tito's here, he can handle the girl."

Duncan appeared too terrified to move, realizing that he'd been duped. When Aviva opened the door, I watched the color drain from his face as he focused on whatever was idling out front.

Jenny's screams, muffled by the gag, rang in my ears. Gunderson seized Levi by the shirt collar and spun him around. Levi let his body go limp and dug the heels of his boots into the ground. Gunderson jerked him up and prodded him forward, but Levi thrusted his legs out. He'd scale the doorframe before marching outside willingly.

"Whoa, we got a bucker here." Gunderson delivered a quick punch to Levi's tailbone, eliciting a groan. "Help me. Now," he said to Duncan.

Duncan inched near me, his hands held out.

I whispered to him, "Fredrich Ernst is dead. And your father is dead too. At the Arbor Day Festival, Aviva and Gunderson argued. Aviva was angry, something about Gunderson making a decision on his own. He murdered Javi. Probably so he could use these sites for the migrants."

Duncan locked eyes with me before grabbing and turning me around. He jabbed an object inside my waistband.

I pawed the object. "What is this?"

Duncan nudged me toward the open door. "Flashlight. I'll try to create a diversion. The rest is up to you."

"To do what?"

"To fight like hell."

And then I saw it. The truck Gunderson had arrived in was a large concrete mixer. Its hydraulic motor hummed, and its drum twisted and agitated. A metal panel jutted out like a boat dock.

Gunderson pushed Levi forward, passing him off to a waiting

Tito Ramirez. Tito was a compact man, but he forcefully shook Levi by the scruff of his neck.

"Looks like we'll finish your museum after all," Aviva said. "The Levi Blue Memorial Museum has a nice ring to it." Then she shoved her gun in my face. "Don't try anything."

"Or what? You'll shoot me?" I scouted the surrounding area, but Duncan was missing. Was this the diversion? But both Duncan and Gunderson were gone.

Gunderson's footsteps came toward us, and he strutted into the glow of a flashlight. He nodded at Tito.

Tito made the sign of the cross. "Adios, cuz."

I sucked in a breath, and my finger searched for the flashlight still snug against my lower back. I focused on breathing.

Do not hyperventilate, I told myself.

"Who wants to take a dip in the cement pond?" Gunderson asked.

Tito jumped into the cab of the truck. I assumed he was our friendly control operator. A few seconds later, concrete spilled down the chute and into the void below us.

"How would a tween boy detective save himself here?" Gunderson pulled Levi up to his feet and muscled him near the hole.

A ground-level flash of brown streaked past Gunderson.

"What the…?" Gunderson's body jerked and gyrated like he'd started to chicken dance. He kicked his leg out, showing that a small dog had firmly attached its mouth to his ankle. "Get it off, get it off." Gunderson lost his balance and stumbled out of my line of vision and into the blackness of the night.

I snapped the flashlight. My fumbling activated some button, and a strobe light blasted out. I jerked it at Aviva, who turned away from the blinding light. I gripped the handle and raised the flashlight from under Aviva's hands, loosening her grip on the gun. She twisted her foot, lost her balance, and thumped to her side.

"Find her gun, find her gun," Levi said, and then dropped to his knees and fumbled for Gunderson's Glock. I searched the ground below me and picked up the pistol that had fallen from Aviva's hands.

Gunderson lurched into the light, his arms raised behind Levi, dutifully playing the monster who just wouldn't die. I threw the flashlight out of my hand to better aim the pistol, my finger pulsing against the trigger. A swinging 2x4, seemingly suspended in midair, obstructed my target and whacked Gunderson across the face.

Tito stuck his head out the truck's window. "What's going on?"

Levi answered his question with the aim of his gun. No stranger to danger, Tito raised his hands in surrender.

I heard a clasp of metal from where Aviva had fallen. Out of the blackness loped Deputy Perkins. I lowered my pistol.

"Good work, Shoe Sho. I'll take it from here." Perkins reached for the Glock.

"Perkins, you magnificent, stone-faced angel," Levi said. "What took you so long?"

In a blink-or-you'd-miss-it moment, the corners of Deputy Perkins's lips twitched.

Chapter 21

"I STILL DON'T UNDERSTAND how this works," I said.

I sat at the lunch counter of the Cherry Blossom Café, watching my sister cut hundreds of tiny pieces of colored paper. She folded each and then dropped them into a bucket.

"You don't have to understand," Jenny said. "It's Levi's bucket list, not yours."

"Fair enough. When do I get mine?"

"Does this mean you'll be sticking around?"

"If you'll have me," I said. "I still have more vacation days to use."

Jenny set down her scissors and scooped up the remaining

pieces of paper. "Vacation days. Is that what we're calling unemployment?"

"Temporary unemployment." I had eventually responded to my hospital administrator's emails, informing her I was relaxing in Texas with my sister. It bought me an extended stay of execution, but I still had to take mandatory therapy sessions if I wanted to return to work. I hadn't decided yet if I did. Jenny and I were communicating better, but I still hadn't discussed the gun incident at the ICU or my prescription drug abuse. Those were conversations for another day.

"You won't have time for your own bucket list, anyway." Jenny slid a mug of matcha my way. "You'll be too busy ticking off the experiences on Levi's."

"Says who?" I asked.

"Says the universe. You two are bonded at the hip."

"Do I have a say in that?"

Jenny cupped her ear. "What's that, universe? No?" She had a glint of mischief in her eyes. "The universe says you get no say. No more Airport Miscellaneous for you. Going forward, it's all miscellaneous."

I sipped my matcha. "I'll schedule a conference call with the universe later to hammer out the details."

Over the next few weeks, Jenny's café was popping with excitement. Motorists who'd normally drive through Bluebonnet Hills on their way to somewhere else were now stopping in for a meal. They came for the gossip, but they stayed for Jenny's amazing food. I sensed most would return, so perhaps she'd make a go of this after all.

"Can I have a cup of coffee, please? Black." Levi hopped backwards into the swivel chair next to me and dropped his head over my matcha.

"Get your own." I pulled the mug toward me.

"How can you drink that with all that gloppy milk in it?" He smacked his tongue against his teeth. "Too much dairy is bad for digestion, and with your sensitive stomach—"

"Are you going to lecture me on dairy intake? Me, the registered nurse?"

Levi shook his head. "Still too sarcastic. I need you more sardonic if this friendship is going to work."

"I'll take my chances."

Jenny presented Levi with his coffee. "Here you are, Mr. Mayor. On the house."

Levi toasted her with the cup.

I shook my head. "I still can't believe you're the mayor."

After Deputy Perkins saved us that night at the construction site, we found that Reverend Duncan Papadopoulos, or Yanni Zepeda, was unconscious from a whack from Gunderson's Glock but thankfully not dead. Unfortunately, Gunderson had murdered Fredrich Ernst and Javi Zepeda and disposed of their bodies in the foundation of the construction site. Levi paid for the retrieval of Fredrich and Javi's bodies and proper burials. The town council appreciated the gesture and asked him to serve as acting mayor. Never one to turn down a great part, Levi accepted.

"Being pretend mayor will be my greatest role yet."

"Acting," I corrected.

"Acting, pretend, we're saying the same thing."

"No, no, we're—"

Jenny ruffled my hair to silence me. "What you two goobers uncovered has got people interested in Bluebonnet Hills again. I've had more customers here this week than I've had since I bought this café." She disappeared through the swinging saloon doors into the kitchen.

Aviva Ernst and Tex Gunderson were taken into custody the night they tried to bury us in cement. Aviva remained tight-lipped, but Gunderson flipped on her quickly. Aviva resented her husband's decision to ditch their DC life for Bluebonnet Hills.

Fearing she'd lost control of her destiny, Aviva pursued the less ambitious Gunderson and pushed him to defraud the town. But Javi Zepeda's loyalty to Fredrich Ernst, and Duncan's loyalty to his father, disrupted her plan. Perhaps she'd appreciate the structure of her new life behind bars.

The person who probably would come out of this best was Tito Ramirez. As a veteran of the judicial system, Tito spilled everything upon arrest, and cut a deal with investigators on the ride to the police station.

"How are you feeling?" I asked my friend once we were alone.

There was some sadness in Levi's eyes that he quickly blinked away. "I'm okay, I'm good. I don't feel any different. That's a good thing, right?"

"A wonderful thing." I patted him on the back.

"Meanwhile, I got a town to run. We need to generate some income. Or I'll go broke."

"And what's first on your agenda, Mr. Mayor?"

Levi fingered the handle of his coffee cup. "Hiring a new chief of police. Preferably one who won't try to kill me."

"Tall order, but I fully support that. You're keeping Deputy Perkins around?"

Levi nodded. "He saved our lives. He loves this town, and the people here trust him. I offered him the police chief position, but he wouldn't accept it, even on an interim basis. He wants to serve the town, not lead it."

We learned Deputy Perkins's suspicions began when he caught five college guys from Austin joyriding through Bluebonnet Hills with a carful of marijuana. Perkins later discovered these guys all had fancy lawyers on retainer, many of whom knew Chief Tex Gunderson. The charges against the boys kept getting reduced until their records practically vanished, yet the crime statistics for Bluebonnet Hills continued to rise. Perkins suspected his commendation for this drug bust was manufactured, explaining his awkwardness at his Arbor Day ceremony. It was my interaction with the spooky, colorful ghosts that motivated him to investigate further.

Perkins conducted an independent search of Aviva Ernst's house after her disappearance and discovered evidence of someone living in a spacious walk-in closet. Namely, he found a two-pound container of protein powder, a set of dumbbells, and a bottle of Nair. It didn't take Agatha Christie to deduce that Gunderson had been hiding out after he'd faked his death and swam across the river.

I finished my matcha and asked Levi, "What about all the partial construction? Any ideas on how you'll finish that?"

Levi sighed. "Barbara Lou Sinclair wants to expand her gym. She's a big aerobics superstar, you know? She wants to build a studio for her videos. We're negotiating a deal for the entire space."

"Good luck. I haven't officially met Barbara Lou, but she strikes me as intense and demanding."

"I agree, you two have a lot in common," Levi quipped. "She also sits on the town council, so I'll certainly see a lot of her."

"You'll have Abilene Schubert to protect you. I am sorry you won't get your museum. I know that was important to you. Now that you're the mayor, I could see that being a huge tourist attraction."

"I'd rather focus on my future, and museums are all about the past. A gym is more practical and will serve more of the residents.... Are you listening?"

I shook my head. "I blacked out when you said *practical*."

"Oh, I'm still scheming. I've devised a way to have a type of museum."

"I'm afraid to ask."

"The mayor's house is huge, too much house for me. So, I'm using two of the downstairs rooms for a no-frills museum. Now, I can pop in from time to time, interact with my public."

"Perhaps for some impromptu miming?"

"Are mayors allowed to mime?"

"Acting mayor, remember? Perhaps you can act like a mayor trapped in an imaginary box."

"Brilliant. When we reboot *Tween of the Crime*, I'm making you head writer." He sipped his coffee. "That dog, the one who saved our lives, did you upload her photo to that neighborhood app?"

"I did, but no one claimed her. I suppose it's for the best. Last time we saw her she was attached to Gunderson's leg."

"We'll meet again soon. She still has a message for me."

The jingle of the bell above the café door rang. Levi gripped my shoulders. "That's our cue, Tanaka-san."

I turned. A woman stood in the doorway. Her braided hair was the color of wheat, and her forest green eyes sparkled as they scanned the room.

"What's happening?" I asked.

"Chief of police interviews. She's our first candidate." Levi waved to catch the woman's attention.

"Are you Mayor Blue?" she asked me.

"No, I'm—"

"Jeepers, creepers, this place is a zoo," she said. "I'm driving into town and there's a car stopped. Right in the middle of the road. And, get this, the guy was taking a picture of his kid in a bunch of bluebonnets. He just got out of his car and plonked his kid into the field to take next year's Christmas card photo. Can you believe that?"

"I'm Mayor Blue." There was a twinkle in Levi's eyes.

"Anyway, sorry I'm late. Oh, my manners are awful. Sorry about that. Also, get used to that." She extended her hand to me. "And are you the mayor's chief of staff?"

Levi laughed. "Yes, yes, he is."

"No, no, I'm not. I'm—"

"Well, nice to meet you. I'm Monday Malone from Lubbock, Texas. And I'm the new chief of police of Bluebonnet Hills." She crossed her fingers. "Hopefully, anyway."

Levi and I beamed at Monday and said in unison, "You're hired!"

About Ryan

Ryan Rivers is the author of the Bucket List Mystery series, featuring Levi Blue and Sho Tanaka.

By day, Ryan teaches technical writing and stops the spread of unnecessary adverbs and vague pronoun references. By mid-afternoon/early evening, he fights crime with his trusty sidekick and toddler son. Together they have uncovered who, in fact, has got your nose and tracked the elusive Peekaboo. They live and eat and occasionally sleep in North Texas with their Brussels griffon pup.

Visit Ryan at http://www.ryanriversbooks.com

Email Ryan at ryan@ryanriversbooks.com

www.ingramcontent.com/pod-product-compliance
Lightning Source LLC
Chambersburg PA
CBHW030635190726
48286CB00008B/2534